Book 1 - Volumes 1-4
or
Slippy and the Sequence of Spontaneous Setbacks

For Sabeena, and our wonderful kids
Amina, Adam, Amir, Aisha and baby
Amelia.

Also, to all the people who helped to
make this story possible; you know who
you are.

Oh, and, thanks Mom!

DEAR SIOBHAN,
I HOPE YOU LIKE
MY BOOKS! PLEASE TELL
ALL YOUR FRIENDS :-)

http://www.adventuresofthesalamander.com

ISBN: 978-0-9857960-0-6

Second Edition

Printed by:
Shenzhen Jinhao Printing Co., Ltd.
http://www.lzjhy.com/

All illustrations by the author, Michael Klaus Schmidt. Text edited and/or proofread by Marlis Schmidt, Tanya Andrious, Frank Tumino and Kerry Schindl.

THE ADVENTURES OF THE SALAMANDER

BOOK I • VOLUMES 1-4
or
Slippy and the Sequence of Spontaneous Setbacks

BOOK II • VOLUMES 5-7
or
Slippy and the Progression of Problematic Predicaments

BOOK III • VOLUMES 8-10
or
Slippy and the Cascade of Curious Confrontations

The Adventures of the Salamander

Volume 1:
Escape From Salamander Village & The River Adventure

THE ADVENTURES OF THE SALAMANDER
by Michael Klaus Schmidt

BOOK I • VOLUME 1

═══════════

Escape From Salamander Village & The River Adventure

Salamander Village was the
wonderful, slimy home of Slippy
the Salamander and his family. The
salamanders were famous for their
yummy cakes and treats.

Chapter 1: Salamander Village

Once upon a time, in the heart of the Olde Forest, there was a village of salamanders. Salamander Village was built amid squishy patches of green moss, where the salamanders had carved their homes out of great mushrooms. Here and there a flower peeked out of its bright petals, and snails made their way slowly from one end of town to the other, involved in their own, mysterious snail business.

The Olde Slimy River ran right through the middle of town, passed under the Slimy River Bridge, and flowed into Salamander Pond. Along the river ran the drainage wall that divided Upper Salamander Village from Lower Salamander Village. It was all quite charming, but just a bit slimy.

All over the forest the salamanders were known for baking wonderful puff pastries, cakes, muffins and other goodies. Every morning they would get up at the crack of dawn and head for the bakery to start a new batch of dough. This took a good part of the morning, and around lunch time a new shift of salamanders would come in to take over.

The second-shift of salamanders would transform the raw dough into all sorts of amazing shapes and forms: spiral pastries that looked like snail shells; long, worm-like, crispy cookies; and any kind of muffin you could imagine, including some that you probably wouldn't want to imagine; they were salamanders, after all. However, the most popular were the purple puff cakes, simple cupcakes with puffy, purple frosting which was just about the best thing in all of the Olde Forest.

That's where Slippy grew up. Slippy was a gentle-hearted salamander boy who could normally be found helping his Mom and Dad in the bakery. Sometimes in his free time he delivered stuff to his neighbors ... when he was not too busy going for a swim or looking for worms, that is.

Of course, not all the salamanders in the village worked in the bakery. There was Mr. Squirmy-Tail the mailman, who delivered everyone's mail once a week. There were Mr. and Mrs. Buggy-Eye the pot makers, who were very skilled in the traditional arts of copper working, and Old Man Axolotl,* who didn't really do much of anything except complain. Finally, and perhaps most importantly, there was Mayor Hellbender,** the largest of all the salamanders, who made sure that everything in the village was kept in working order.

Salamander Village was a quiet and peaceful place to live ... until one day, when a mysterious hooded stranger ran down River Road and across the bridge, shouting, "The Lizards are Coming! The Lizards are Coming!" While startled for a moment, everyone in town soon laughed about the incident and went on with their daily routine without giving the odd stranger a second thought.

Chapter 2: The Lizard Invasion

All the wonderful pastries and cakes, the hospitality of the salamanders, as well as their charming homes, brought many visitors to Salamander Village. Creatures from all around the Olde Forest and beyond came to buy cakes and muffins, and for many years the salamanders were the envy of the forest. All of that changed the day the lizards arrived, just a week after the village had turned a deaf ear to the mysterious stranger's warnings.

---

* An Axolotl is a strange salamander with gills on the outside of its neck.
** The Hellbender, at over two feet long, is one of the world's largest amphibians

One day, a strange salamander ran through Salamander Village yelling, "The Lizards are Coming!" Everyone thought he was crazy.

The lizards were the salamanders' bigger, greener, and scalier cousins. They loved to be in control ... and now, totally unexpected by anyone, they had decided that they wanted Salamander Village for themselves, and that they would force the salamanders to bake for them.

Once they arrived, the lizards were knocking on doors, waiting patiently until the unsuspecting salamanders came out. When they did, the lizards would grab them and force them over to the bakery to start working. If no one answered the door, the lizards would break it down and take any salamanders inside by force.

The very next week, lizards really did attack Salamander Village. They made the salamanders bake for them. Slippy was kicked out of his own house!

Our young friend Slippy happened to be home alone that day. Amidst the turmoil and chaos, Slippy thought it best to get out. He only had enough time to pack his little travelling bag with some cheese, carefully wrapping it in wax paper, before he was pushed out of his home by a particularly mean and nasty lizard named Grumpus.

Once outside he could not believe his eyes. The huge lizards were pushing the poor little salamanders towards the bakery. Slippy didn't even have a chance to look for his family.

When Slippy, who was not the type to just take abuse like this, decided to say something about it, Grumpus simply clubbed him on the head with his stick, and Slippy fell to the ground, unconscious.

Slippy woke up all alone. It was dark and wet, and he had no idea where he was. He found his bag with the cheese still in it, but the bag was damp, and this did not improve Slippy's mood at all. Nor did the bump on his head. As his eyes adjusted to

Slippy was put in jail for speaking out against the lizards; it was not fair. All he wanted to do was help his family and friends.

Slippy escaped from the jail and sneaked out of Salamander Village. Lizards were looking for him all over; he was really scared.

the dim light, he found that he was in a small cell with one tiny window that was barred up. The lizards had imprisoned him! Fortunately for Slippy, the lizards had built this cell for something about the size and shape of a lizard. Lizards are dry and scaly and rather bulky compared to the smooth and slimy salamanders. It took no time at all for Slippy to slip through the bars and escape his cell.

Once outside, Slippy saw about a dozen wagons holding more jail cells, exactly like the one from which he had just escaped. Unfortunately, though, quite a few lizards were guarding the prison compound, several of them standing nearby. Slippy didn't have time to think about who might be in the other cells, and by the time the lizards realized what had happened, he was off and running.

A great chase ensued, and the whole village was mobilized. Lizards were looking for Slippy everywhere. Around every corner more lizard search parties were running to and fro. Slippy knew that the fastest way out of town was through the main gate, but it would be heavily guarded. Salamander Pond was the only way of escape. Lizards are not at home in the water, and Slippy thought he would have the advantage there.

Realizing that his home wasn't safe anymore, Slippy darted over Slimy River Bridge and along the top of the drainage wall, right to the edge of Salamander Pond ... he'd made it! He took a deep breath and felt good about his narrow escape. However, he started to think about the other salamanders in the village. How could he leave when his parents, his older brother, his younger sister and his friends were all locked up and being forced to bake for the lizards? Looking back, he saw smoke and steam rise from the bakery. Even at this late hour, members of his family might be mixing dough, melting chocolate, or baking puff cakes. He couldn't just stand by and let this happen; he had to do something!

Slippy decided to go back. It would be difficult, what with all the lizards out on the hunt, but go he must. He would have to stay in the shadows, hiding behind shrubs and fences and crawling under porches. Slippy jumped down from the river wall and swam across the Olde Slimy River. He hopped out on the opposite side and crossed River Road. From all different directions he could hear shouts: the search parties, still looking for him, no doubt. Slippy hopped the fence into the Caecilians'* (pronounced see-sil-yenz) backyard, then crawled

* Caecilians are unusual, legless, burrowing amphibians.

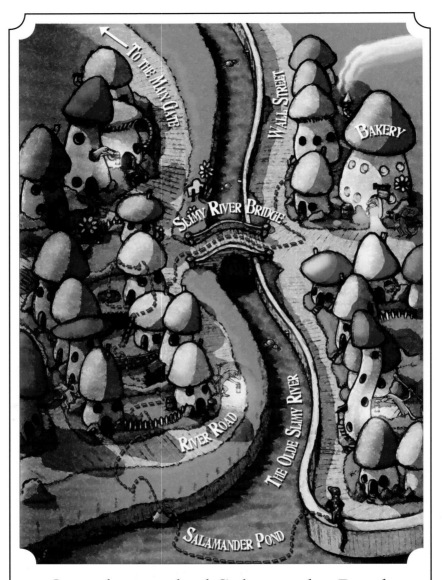

Once he reached Salamander Pond, Slippy stopped and looked back. He decided he had to go back and rescue the salamanders trapped in the bakery.

under the hedge and waited under Old Man Axolotl's back porch until the shouting subsided. When he could hear nothing more, he quietly crawled out and climbed over the wall into Mr. and Mrs. Newt's backyard.

The next house over was Slippy's own; he knew he wouldn't be able to hop the fence. It was too tall and had sharp points on top. So he climbed a ladder onto the Newts' roof and, with a running start, leapt over onto the roof of his own house. From there he jumped down into a pool of water in the backyard. Cautiously, he entered the house through the back door and used the bathroom (he had needed to go ever since he woke up in that jail cell).

Carefully peeking out from his front door, he had a good view of the bridge and the upper village where the bakery was located. Waiting a while to catch his breath, he noticed lizard guards crossing the bridge every 10 minutes or so. After the third set of guards had passed, he made his move. He ran out the front door and right over the bridge from where he could clearly see the front doors of the bakery. Two lizards were there, standing guard. Slippy realized that it was going to be more difficult than he'd thought.

Chapter 3: The Bakery

Slippy cautiously managed to sneak around to one of the bakery's many windows. Inside, he could see some of his fellow salamanders, looking tired and worried, baking honey cakes and banana muffins. Slippy could not see any lizards, but he saw someone who looked just like his brother ... it was his brother, Sloppy! Sloppy had just taken a whole tray of puff cakes out of the oven, and when he thought no one was looking, he took a bite out of one.

Suddenly a lizard appeared out of an adjacent room, quickly came over and smacked Sloppy, taking the tray of cakes from him.

"Cakes are for lizards! Remember that!" yelled the lizard, and "There's plenty of dried bread and warm water for you after your shift is over!"

Slippy cringed, "How awful!" he thought. "Everyone knows that salamanders hate warm water!"

The situation seemed hopeless, but just then a familiar face came up right behind the window, looking at him. It was his mother!

"Hi, Mom!" said Slippy.

"Sssshhhhhh!" said his mother. "It's too dangerous here; you really must get out of town; they're looking for you."

"Mom," whispered Slippy, "I want to help you escape!"

"No," said his mother, "it's too risky; there are too many guards."

His mother continued, "They are forcing us to bake for them, but otherwise we're safe. Your father and Sloppy are here with me in the bakery, and they have your sister Sally working in the advertising department. If you want to help us, you can't do it alone." She explained, "They're putting the 'troublemakers' in those cages; maybe you could release some of them."

She was right, of course; if the cages where he had been held

At the bakery, Slippy saw his mom and his brother Sloppy, along with others. His mother told him to leave the village and find help.

were not empty, that's where he'd have to start.

"Thanks, Mom!" whispered Slippy, a tear in his eye.

"I love you son!" whispered his mom.

While all the lizards were still out searching for him in the village and investigating the forest, they never thought he might come back to the cages. As a result, they had left only one lazy lizard to guard them. However, they had also boarded up the

Slippy went to help the other salamanders escape from jail. Luckily, only one lazy lizard was guarding them. Slippy took the keys and unlocked the doors.

windows so no other salamanders could slip out. The guard, whose name was Reginald, had fallen asleep while on duty, a key ring dangled on the end of his tail.

After carefully snatching the key while trying not to breathe too loud, Slippy quickly opened up all the cells, releasing the imprisoned salamanders. Hushed greetings were exchanged, and everybody was relieved, but there was no time to lose; they had to get out of the village quickly.

On their way to Salamander Pond, they ran along the top of the drainage wall that ran along Wall Street. Slippy slipped on a wet patch of moss and fell off the wall. In their fear and haste, the other salamanders did not notice his absence and went on without him. Slippy was alone, unconscious, and wet ... again!

When he awoke, Slippy found that dawn was approaching. The lizards had not yet found him. The pain in the back of his head made him realize that he must have been knocked out once more. Making his way slowly and carefully in the dim light, he had no idea where any of the other salamanders

The other salamanders escaped, but Slippy slipped and fell into the river with a splash.

After he woke up, Slippy finally escaped to Salamander Pond, where he climbed on a rock and fell asleep. He thought about how he could save his village ... tomorrow!

had gone. Not about to waste any more time, though, he decided to get away from the village to safety before worrying about them.

Once he got to Salamander Pond, he swam as quietly as he could towards an island. It was more of a rock, really, but it looked like it might be far enough from the village not to be seen, and large enough for him to rest and to plan his next move. Slippy stayed behind the rock for a while, checking out his surroundings.

As the light of morning grew, a mist arose from the pond. Slippy realized it would be safe to climb on the rock to get some rest; the mist would serve to hide him from the eyes of the lizards in the village. Slippy, exhausted from the previous night's activities, imagined that he would finally do something about those lizards, right after getting some well deserved rest.

Chapter 4: Tortoises, Turtles & Terrapins

After having a few mouthfuls of cheese, Slippy decided that he should come up with a plan to save his village. From his lookout on the rock, he could see that Salamander Village was completely overrun by lizards. Realizing how dangerous it would be to return home, he began thinking out loud, "What am I going to do?"

This is what salamanders do when they're alone and under pressure. What Slippy did not expect was to hear an answer.

"You could start by giving me some of that cheese. It smells delicious," said a mysterious voice.

Just inches from his face, Slippy saw the head and neck of a large reptile rising out of the water. Thinking it was another lizard, Slippy got up, covered his face in a panic, and started begging, "Please, Mr. Lizard, please don't eat me!"

The creature responded by saying, "I'm neither a lizard, nor do I want to eat you. But I wouldn't mind, in case you didn't hear me before, I wouldn't mind trying some of that cheese."

"Well, if you're not a lizard, then what are you?" asked Slippy. "You're clearly some form of reptilian ...?"

"That I am," responded the reptile, "I happen to be what you would call a 'terrapin.'"

"I've never heard of a terrapin!" said Slippy. "Is that like a lizard?"

"No," said the terrapin, "lizards don't have shells, and, as you can see, I have a shell."

Slippy looked askance at the terrapin, wondering what in the world it was talking about. "A shell?" he asked. "All I can see is your head and a bit of your neck."

The terrapin laughed, "You're standing on it!"

Slippy looked down, and, sure enough, the rock he thought he was sitting on was indeed the shell of the terrapin. It shifted under him ever so slightly, and he realized that they were float-ing on the water. Seeing the creature from this angle, with the shell and neck and head together, he knew exactly what it was; "Oh! I see ... you are a turtle!

"No! No! No! I am not a turtle!" The terrapin seemed angry;

The rock that Slippy had climbed
on was not a rock, at all. It was
a terrapin named Sheldon. They
decided to go to Sheldon's home to
ask his family for help.

"How can people be so insensitive?" it lamented. "They think we're all the same."

"I'm sorry," said Slippy, "you look like a turtle."

The terrapin lifted one of his great clawed forelegs from the water, menacing Slippy. "If I were a turtle, would I have this?"

Tortoise

Terrapin

Turtle

Sheldon explained that terrapins, like him, are different from turtles and tortoises, but everyone calls them all turtles, anyway.

it cried.

Slippy was dumbfounded; he did not know what to say.

"No, I suppose it's not your fault," said the terrapin finally. "Obviously, no one has ever explained the difference to you."

"I suppose not," hesitated Slippy, still not sure of what to make of all this.

"Let me explain," said the terrapin. "There are three main types of shelled reptiles, or chelonians*," it continued, "the tortoise, who lives strictly on land; the turtle, who lives in the ocean and has flippers, not feet ... flippers!" It was getting angry again.

"Sorry, it just makes me so mad when the turtles get all the credit ... anyway, the turtles live in the sea, salt water that is, and they don't have feet or claws; they have flippers. Finally, we terrapins, we live in and around lakes and rivers. Fresh water: you see the difference now? And we have feet, webbed feet, with claws ... see?"

The terrapin was waving his clawed foot around again, as if to demonstrate. Slippy was still confused a bit, but he understood why the terrapin might get offended. Then Slippy thought about it, and imagined someone calling him a toad or a newt. Suddenly, it all made sense.

"I understand," he said finally, "you're a terrapin, not a turtle and not a tortoise ... a terrapin."

"Yes, you've got it!" the terrapin smiled.

Slippy explained, "You see, where I'm from, we call all of the shelled reptiles 'turtles' ... imagine! I meant no offense."

"I suppose not," answered the terrapin, "everyone does it ... my name's Sheldon, by the way."

"Nice to meet you, Sheldon, I'm Slippy," said Slippy.

Sheldon and Slippy shook hands; they became great friends right then and there. Slippy shared some of his cheese with him and told him about the lizards and what had happened in

* According to *Funk & Wagnall's Wildlife Encyclopedia, Volume 2,* p. 191, 1974 Edition.

Salamander Village.

Sheldon listened with great interest; then he exclaimed, "That's too bad about the lizards, by the way, I love your people's pastries!" After a short pause, he exclaimed, "I have an idea!"

"What is it?" asked Slippy.

Sheldon explained that his family lived on an island. The Olde Slimy River, Slippy was surprised to learn, continued on the other side of Salamander Pond and flowed into The Great Lazy River, which wound through the Farmlands and into Bog Bottom Bay.

"Apparently," explained Sheldon, "if you swim deep enough, you will find the bottom of Bog Bottom Bay to be covered with a thick gooey substance. I've never been to the bottom myself, but I was told that it was very dangerous because you could get stuck in the goo and never come out."

Sheldon continued, "Anyway, in the middle of the bay is an island, Golden Leaf Island, where my family lives. It was named after the beautiful golden leaves that grow on the trees there. My idea is to go find my family and the other terrapins on the island and ask for help."

Slippy said, "That sounds like a fine idea, Sheldon." And without delay they were travelling down the river.

Chapter 5: The Bobcat's Idea

After travelling down the Southern branch of the Olde Slimy River for a while, they came to the Great Lazy River. Slippy

On the way to Sheldon's home on Golden Leaf Island, Slippy learned that Salamander Village was part of a big world that he had never known about.

They travelled down the Olde Slimy River to the Great Lazy River. Slippy noticed how much cleaner its water was compared to the Olde Slimy River.

was really impressed by its great width, and even more by its fresh, clear water. He had grown up near Salamander Pond, which had nothing but dark, murky waters. Sheldon explained that most of the rivers and ponds were clear and bluish in color.* Slippy stared into the depths of the river, surprised to be able to see straight through to the bottom. Occasionally, he looked up to see the farm houses slowly drifting by, but he spent most of his time looking down. That explains why he didn't see the really big, hungry bobcat that was following

* Water is not actually blue, but can appear so when it reflects a blue sky.

them from behind, along the river bank.

The bobcat had noticed Sheldon and Slippy drifting down the river and had thought about how lovely it would be to have breakfast and lunch served at the same time. Should he have the turtle for breakfast, and the salamander for lunch? Or should he have the salamander for breakfast, and the turtle for lunch? He was not sure, but he loved the idea of having both options. The bobcat decided, then and there, to call this new meal "brunch."

Amazed at his own cleverness, he noticed his mouth starting to water. The only thing the bobcat would have loved more than reptiles and amphibians for a snack would have been cheese. He was deep in thoughts about cheese when he stepped on a twig, and the ensuing "snap" caused Slippy to look up and take notice.

Slippy didn't know what a bobcat was, so he had no idea that it posed any sort of danger. He decided to ask Sheldon. "Sheldon?" he asked.

"Yes?" said Sheldon.

"Have you ever seen a big, fuzzy creature with two fuzzy, pointy things on its head?" asked Slippy.

"Sure," said Sheldon, "those are mammals, and those things on their head, well, we call those 'ears.'"

Sheldon couldn't see the bobcat, so he thought that Slippy was just asking questions out of curiosity.

"Mammals ... hmmm! Are there different sorts of mammals, Sheldon?" continued Slippy.

Along the way, Slippy and Sheldon met a bobcat. Slippy thought the bobcat was friendly, but it really just wanted to eat them both.

"Oh sure," said Sheldon, "lots of them."

The bobcat was drawing near, getting ready to pounce.

Getting slightly concerned, Slippy decided to go into more detail. "What would you call one with a flat, fuzzy sort of face, long hairs sticking out of its upper lip, long pointy teeth, and a short little stumpy tail?" he asked.

"That," answered Sheldon, "sounds like a bobcat."

"Hello, Mr. Bobcat!" shouted Slippy, waving at the beast.

"What?!" cried Sheldon. He turned around and saw the creature approach rapidly. He tried to swim faster, but it was too late. The bobcat pounced, scooped both Slippy and Sheldon out of the river, and pinned the two friends against the bank, one under each paw.

"Well, well, well, well, well, what do we have here? A salamander and a turtle." said the bobcat in his flowery, sarcastic manner. "One for breakfast, one for lunch!" The bobcat thought he was being very ironic.

Slippy still didn't understand what was happening, never having been threatened by a sarcastic bobcat before. Thinking he was just being friendly and inviting them to eat together, Slippy exclaimed, "Oh, I wish I had brought more than just cheese!"

Sheldon was astounded, "A bobcat is about to have us for brunch, and you're worried about your cheese? And, by the way," he scowled at the bobcat, "I'm a terrapin!"

The bobcat's brain could not handle all the conflicting incoming data. He wanted to know about the cheese, for sure, but he was also curious about how the turtle, er ... terrapin, knew about "brunch." Were these two creatures reading his mind? Was this all part of some twisted, cold-blooded plot to drive him mad? The bobcat grew fearful but, looking at the two of them, decided that he was too hungry to worry about it.

"Did you say ... cheese?" he asked, his stomach winning out in the end.

Sheldon was very perceptive and saw that the bobcat, although larger and stronger than either Slippy or himself, seemed to actually be somewhat afraid of them. Taking advantage of this, he said in a very stern voice, "Yes, we have the cheese. But you will neither see it, nor smell it, unless you unhand us at once!"

Sheldon's plan worked. The bobcat was truly frightened now, especially when he realized the terrapin not only knew about brunch but also about his secret love for cheese.

"Er ... yes, Sir!" he replied and immediately let them go.

The bobcat was mean and scary, but Sheldon figured out that it really liked cheese. Luckily, Slippy had cheese with him, in his bag.

Sheldon finally convinced the Bobcat
to eat some cheese, instead of Slippy
and himself.

Sheldon noticed that the bobcat was now shaking with fear, so
he continued even louder, pointing a clawed finger at the bobcat's nose, "Right! Now my friend here will provide you with
the cheese, but you need to go back to your people and warn
them not to bother us terrapins and salamanders any more, or
there will be grave consequences. Do you understand?"

The Bobcat was relieved; he could escape with his life and have
some cheese, too. "Thank you, Sir," he groveled.

He took the cheese that Slippy handed him and skulked off, back towards the woods, wondering whether it was wise to actually eat the cheese given to him by such a suspicious pair of creatures. The question of "brunch" would have to remain a mystery; the bobcat was too afraid to go back and ask them about it.

Chapter 6: Lunch

After their encounter with the bobcat and all that talk about food, Slippy and Sheldon realized they were hungry. Nothing was more pressing for them to do but find some lunch. The cheese they had left would be nice for a snack but do little to satisfy lunchtime cravings. However, since there was nothing for them to eat in the middle of the river, they decided to stop at the next farm to see if they could acquire some food.

The next farm, as it turned out, belonged to a middle-aged hedgehog couple by the name of Mr. and Mrs. Bristlebottom. Mrs. Bristlebottom was just about the most hospitable hostess along the entirety of the Great Lazy River. Mrs. Bristlebottom - Doris was her name - was the type of hedgehog who always expected company, even when no company was expected. This made Herbert, her husband, get somewhat grumpy from time to time. "You're wasting food, Doris!" he would say. Of course, she never actually wasted the food; she would always find some use for it, distributing it among the other forest creatures or serving it later as leftovers.

As they approached the farm, Slippy and Sheldon noticed how tidy everything was. Neat rows of shrubs lined the front yard, and a lovely thatched roof covered the home like a blanket. Round windows and a wide door indicated that the inhabitants might be of the plump variety.

Amazingly, Mrs. Bristlebottom had just prepared a whole table of delicious food when Slippy and Sheldon wearily knocked on the door. "Come in, come in!" she said, to their surprise. Doris behaved as if she had been expecting them all along and they had just arrived a few minutes late.

This made Slippy and Sheldon slightly nervous, as if it were too good to be true. However, when they saw the food, their doubts started to fade away quickly. They were so hungry, they started eating almost immediately, and when they saw Mr. and Mrs. Bristlebottom eating along with them, they could not even remember having had doubts in the first place.

Now the lunch was not what most of us would consider to be wonderful or delicious, but we must remember that hedgehogs, terrapins and salamanders have slightly different diets than the rest of us. As an appetizer, they ate deep-fried breaded mealworm doodles, which are crunchy on the outside and gooey on the inside. Of course, you can't serve deep-fried breaded mealworm doodles without a dip, so Mrs. Bristlebottom had prepared a lovely sauce of snail slime and chopped mushroom stalks.

Then they were served the second course, which consisted of mashed dandelion roots, with butter, of course, and sauteed cricket legs, or "cricket sticks," as they are called.

Slippy was quite full from all the food but noticed that Mr. Bristlebottom wasn't eating as much as the others. He looked over at Slippy, winked and said, "You have to pace yourself."

Just then Mrs. Bristlebottom brought out the main course, a whole roasted slug (prepared with a dash of salt, pepper, lemon and a hint of swamp scum), peas, carrots and corn. It was the most delicious dish Slippy had ever eaten, though he soon realized he shouldn't have eaten quite so much of it. For dessert, Mrs. Bristlebottom had prepared some roly-poly pudding (made from real roly-poly bugs) and some puff pastries she had bought earlier that week in Salamander Village.

When Slippy saw the pastries, he almost choked on his cricket

They stopped for lunch at the home of two very nice hedgehogs, Doris and Herbert Bristlebottom. There they ate mashed dandelion roots, snail slime sauce, cricket sticks, deep-fried breaded mealworm doodles and ...

... a whole roasted slug ... yummy!

stick. "What's the matter?" cried Mr. Bristlebottom.

Over pudding and pastries and a steaming cup of tea, with Slippy sobbing uncontrollably, Sheldon told the Bristlebottoms the story of how the lizards had taken over Salamander Village and what had happened to Slippy's family. He also mentioned his plan of getting help from the rest of the terrapins.

Mrs. Bristlebottom was very distraught, both due to the injustice done to the salamanders ... and because she had planned to pick up some muffins that very afternoon.

"Something must be done!" she stated angrily, with a look of determination on her face. Rolling pin in hand, she made for the door as if she were going to teach those lizards a lesson right then and there.

"No, wait!" cried Slippy. "We need to get more help. There are many lizards in the village, and there are too few of us, still." It was difficult, but they managed to convince Mrs. Bristlebottom to listen to reason.

They finally agreed that Slippy and Sheldon were to return to the Bristlebottoms as soon as they were ready to head back to the village and face the lizards. The Bristlebottoms promised to tell all their friends about the tragedy at Salamander Village and to be ready for the day they came back. Slippy and Sheldon departed with full stomachs, a bag filled with leftovers and two new, powerful allies in the struggle against lizard tyranny.

Chapter 7: Trouble at Bog-Bottom Bay

The rest of their river journey was quite uneventful. Slippy and Sheldon floated along, content to drift with the current. They stopped once in the evening when they got hungry to snack on some leftovers.

It was getting dark, and Slippy thought it would be a good idea to camp for the night. Sheldon, however, said that they were almost at Bog-Bottom Bay, and they could easily make it to his home in time for supper if they continued.

Bog-Bottom Bay looked peaceful enough when they finally floated out of the mouth of the Great Lazy River. They could see the lights on Golden Leaf Island through the fog that was rising off the surface of the bay.

Mrs. Bristlebottom was very nice
and wanted to help Slippy save his
village. After lunch, and tea, she
filled Slippy's bag with food to take
along on his trip.

About halfway between the river mouth and the island
Slippy, wishing he hadn't eaten so much, stood up on Sheldon's shell in order to stretch. At the very same moment Sheldon felt something, probably a water weed, brush against one
of his legs. It startled Sheldon, causing him to squirm, which
then caused Slippy to let out a little screech, lose his balance,
and fall right into the bay with a splash! He was underwater
for only a few moments, and it was easy enough for him to

When they got to Bog-Bottom Bay, Slippy fell off of Sheldon's shell and into the dark water. Slippy got out safely, but his bag sank to the bottom, so Sheldon swam down after it.

climb back onto Sheldon's shell. However, when he sat down again, he noticed his travelling bag was missing.

"My bag!" cried Slippy. "I must have dropped my bag."

Sure enough, the bag was at that very moment sinking slowly to the bottom of the bay, right into the goo. Fearing the rest of their leftovers would be lost forever, Sheldon dove after it. He could see the bag, deep below him, almost invisible in the darkness of the boggy bottom.

As Sheldon swam down after the bag, Slippy tried calling him, reminding him about the dangers of the goo, but his pleading could not be heard underwater.

Sheldon was aware of the dangers of the goo, but he thought if he dove fast enough, he would not have to worry about getting stuck. He was wrong! By the time he reached the bag, it had already settled into the thick goo at the bottom of the bay. He tried pulling it up, but it was impossible. In fact, he didn't realize it, but the bag was actually, almost imperceptibly, pulling him down into the boggy goo with it. Soon his foot was stuck in the goo. Sheldon struggled with the bag until the whole upper half of his body was caught in the thick, dark substance. He called for help, but only bubbles emerged from the thick goo.

Slippy frantically swam, as quickly as he could, towards the island, yelling at the top of his lungs. He knew he could not pull Sheldon out of the goo alone, but perhaps the terrapins could help. When he reached the shore, some of Sheldon's family members were already standing near the water. They had heard the shouting, and since Slippy had used Sheldon's name, they were very concerned as they helped him onto land.

"The bog! ... Sheldon ... Roasted Slug!" were the first words that stuttered out of his mouth. Nevertheless, the terrapins seemed to understand. "It's Sheldon; he's in trouble!" shouted one, while another quickly jumped into the water, swimming out in the direction towards which Slippy was pointing. They saw the bubbles from Sheldon's cries for help rise to the surface and knew they were at the right place.

Sheldon's brothers Willy and Bernhard dove down into the

Sheldon got stuck in the bottom, but his brothers were close. They pulled him out of the goo at the bottom of Bog-Bottom Bay. The bag was lost.

darkness. When they reached the bottom, all they could see was the tip of Sheldon's tail.

Fortunately, Sheldon's older brothers had done this sort of thing before. Willy grabbed Sheldon's tail while Bernard grabbed Willy's tail, and both pulled as hard as they could. With their combined strength, they were able to get Sheldon free of the goo, before it was too late.* But the bag was lost ... another victim of the dark waters of Bog-Bottom Bay.

---

* Fortunately, terrapins can hold their breath for long periods of time.

Chapter 8: Golden Leaf Island

Terrapin Hall, as it was called, was a wide, low structure made of hollowed-out logs It spread out in all different directions because all of Sheldon's brothers, once they had reached maturity and started their own families, had added their own wing to the building. Sheldon was young and still lived in his parents' area of the home.

The main dining hall was where all the families would meet for meals, and this is where they now brought Slippy and Sheldon, cold, wet and exhausted, in order to feed them and warm them up after their ordeal.

The hall had a large hearth in the center, and the fire roared, warming the whole room. Towels were distributed by smiling terrapins, along with great steaming mugs of hot punch. Slippy thought that suffering through the cold and wet bog was almost worth it. The punch, the warmth and the friendly terrapin faces certainly took the edge off of any pain he still felt.

After supper and after many cheerful introductions, Slippy had a chance to tell Sheldon's family about the plight of Salamander Village. All the terrapins were concerned and admitted that they had no idea lizards could be so vicious. However, they were not able to commit to going back with Slippy. Not because they didn't want to, mind you, but because Mr. Schumacher was not home. All major decisions, like this one, were made by the Schumacher Family's father and leader.

"He's not far, though ..." said Willy. It turned out Mr. Schumacher had travelled to the other side of Golden Leaf Island to trade with the merchants who came from all over the world.

Slippy was surprised to find out that Bog-Bottom Bay was just a small body of water that opened up into the Great Blue-Green Ocean. He had never known that his little Salamander Pond was connected to such an immense world.

They would go first thing in the morning (after breakfast, of course), across Golden Leaf Island to find Sheldon's father. But for now they would rest. And as Lucinda, one of Sheldon's sisters, passed around some lovely homemade brownies, Slippy began to get drowsy. After that day's adventures, he really needed a long, long nap ... and that's just what he got.

When they reached Golden Leaf Island, Slippy and Sheldon were given mugs of hot punch, and then they rested in front of a warm fire.

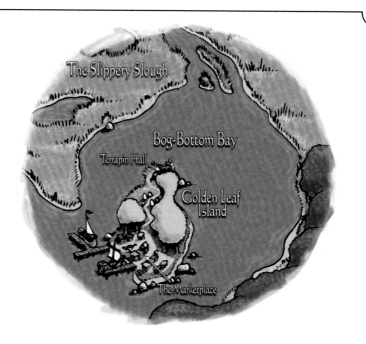

The next day, Sheldon and Slippy were going to look for Sheldon's father on the other side of the island. Then, he might help them save Salamander Village ... but that's another story.

Slippy fell asleep thinking about how he would return to Salamander Village in the morning. He would come with an army of terrapins to save his family from the lizards.

Little did he know ... but that's another story.

The Adventures of the Salamander

Volume 2: Sailing the Great Blue-Green Ocean

THE ADVENTURES OF THE SALAMANDER
by Michael Klaus Schmidt

BOOK I • VOLUME 2

Sailing The Great Blue-Green Ocean

After getting away from the lizards in Salamander Village, Slippy and his new friend Sheldon travelled down the Great Lazy River.

After a long day, they finally got to Sheldon's home on Golden Leaf Island. There, they slept safe and sound.

Chapter 1: The Naturalist

As you remember, Slippy the Salamander had been able to escape from Salamander Village where he was in great danger. A group of mean-spirited lizards had moved into his tranquil village, taken over its famous bakery and went about forcing Slippy's family and the other salamanders to bake for them.

On his way out of town, Slippy had met Sheldon the terrapin. Together they travelled down river to Golden Leaf Island, where Sheldon's family lived, to ask for help. As it turned out, Mr. Schumacher, Sheldon's father, had gone to the market-place on the other side of Golden Leaf Island.

Sheldon and Slippy decided to take a trip across the island to find him, first thing in the morning. After a good night's rest, they had a large breakfast of hot pancakes with thick maple syrup that Sheldon's mother and older brother, Willy, had prepared for them. They set out at a good pace, bringing along a new bag of goodies for the journey, Slippy's travelling bag having been lost at the bottom of Bog-Bottom Bay and all. As they walked in the cool ocean breeze, they spoke about their favorite foods, and later Sheldon brought up all the different creatures he had encountered on his journeys.

"I'm somewhat of a naturalist," said Sheldon.

"Really?" asked Slippy. "What does a naturalist do?"

"A naturalist studies the many forms of life in this wonderful world in which we live," explained Sheldon.

Slippy was impressed, "How many forms of life are there?"

The trail sloped upwards; a green hill rose before them. "Oh, too many to count," continued Sheldon. "But we try to break it all down by classifying them into groups and such. There are four main groups ... 'Kingdoms,' we call them."

Slippy thought he had heard about kingdoms before, but he thought he remembered there being five*. "What are these four Kingdoms?" asked Slippy, curious to hear Sheldon's explanation.

"Oh, that's easy," said Sheldon, going on, "there's the Fungus Kingdom, you know, mushrooms, toadstools ... and that fuzzy stuff you find on your bread after a few days."

"Oh yeah!" Slippy complained, "I ate a muffin once with some of that stuff on it and had the worst stomach ache for days!"

"It can do that," agreed Sheldon.

They reached the top of the hill, which was crowned with a ring of huge white stones, the other side of the island stretching out below them. In the distance they could see the sails of many ships, indicating a harbor of some sort. It seemed a great crowd of people was moving around among the many multicolored tents and tables set up along the shore.

Sheldon continued, "Then there's the Plant Kingdom with its trees, water lilies, daisies and squishy mosses. I love plants, but not as much as I like the Animal Kingdom. Animals are quite amazing, able to do all sorts of feats ... we are animals, you know."

"You don't say!" responded Slippy.

* Slippy was right; there are actually five Kingdoms in biological classification - or six, depending on whom you ask..

54

Slippy and Sheldon woke up the next morning. They set out across Golden Leaf Island to find Mr. Schumacher, Sheldon's father, at the marketplace.

"Sure do," said Sheldon, "we and anything else that crawls, slithers, swims or flies through this amazing world. From the worms under your feet to the squids in the sea, the birds in the air, and the bugs, lizards, hedgehogs, snakes, gophers and salamanders we see every day. Then there are the chimeras ..."

"Chimeras?" asked Slippy, never having heard the term.

"Oh yes, the chimeras are those mixtures of different types of animals. You see, animals have their own classifications too, but sometimes certain animals, the chimeras, mysteriously

Along the way, Sheldon told Slippy about all the kinds of life in the world: the fungi, the plants, the animals ... and the chimeras (things that combine more than one animal form, like dragons).

decide not to stay within their proper classification; they take parts from all sorts of other animals and muck them together into one. No one knows why this happens. It's one of the great mysteries."

They were walking under a canopy of trees, which blotted out the light from the sun almost completely, but the path was straight, and Sheldon seemed to know the way.

Curious to hear more, Slippy asked, "What kinds of things are these chimeras?"

"Oh, you've heard of them, I'm sure," said Sheldon. "The dragons are the most famous, a combination of bats and snakes and lions. I've never seen one of those, but my uncle told me about one that he saw as a kid. And the basilisk, a snake with a rooster's head. They say it will kill anyone who looks at it. Oh, and there's the Pegasus, a horse with the wings of an eagle; beautiful creatures, I'm told. Not to mention the gryphons, bixies, and the dreaded Krak-o-pod. Of course, as a scientist I'm sure there's a logical explanation for these things' existence; we just haven't discovered it yet."

Slippy wondered if Sheldon was being serious and inquired further, "Have you ever seen one of these chimeras?"

"Oh yes. We're probably going to see one today at the market-place," said Sheldon, "one of the strangest chimeras of all ... the platypus."

Chapter 2: The Marketplace

When they finally arrived at the marketplace, lo and behold, standing in front of them was the strangest creature Slippy had ever seen. It looked almost like a beaver, but in place of a beaver's whiskered nose was a big bill, like that of a duck. Its feet were webbed, and its tail was flat. It looked at them, standing motionless ... and suddenly broke out in a broad smile.

When they reached the marketplace, Slippy met Mr. Bigsby, a platypus, who was friends with Sheldon and his family. He told them that Sheldon's Dad was on a boat called the Sea Serpent.

"Sheldon Schumacher! As I live and breathe!" cried the unusual creature; apparently, it knew Sheldon.

"Hey, Mr. Bigsby!" shouted Sheldon, clearly recognizing him.

Sheldon introduced them; "Mr. Bigsby, this is Slippy."

"A pleasure to meet you, my boy!" Mr. Bigsby and Slippy shook hands, a very hearty handshake to be sure. Slippy was beginning to feel it would never end.

Sheldon broke in with an explanation: "We're looking for my father."

Mr. Bigsby released Slippy's hand, much to Slippy's relief, and responded, "Oh yes, I saw your father just a few minutes ago. He was on the "Sea Serpent," picking out some fine Eastern

Mr. Bigsby was a platypus, a type of chimera that has the body and tail of a beaver, but the feet and bill of a duck.

rugs." Mr. Bigsby was pointing past the tents, stands and people of the marketplace at a tall sailing ship that had gone unnoticed by Slippy. Sheldon's father was a merchant who served the local community. He regularly came to the marketplace to buy from the trading ships, which arrived about once a month.

"Come, I'll help you find your father," said Mr. Bigsby. "What's the emergency?"

Sheldon explained the sad story of Salamander Village to Mr. Bigsby who, as Slippy learned, apparently ran the inn just off the docks. Mr. Bigsby nodded and made sympathetic noises, his brow furrowed with concern.

"Well, your father will definitely want to know about this," said Mr. Bigsby, "but I wouldn't recommend you turtles trying this alone. I've seen lizards at work before, and they're nothing to trifle with."

Sheldon ignored the comment about turtles. As they made their way to the ship, they seemed to walk into a different world. Slippy could see all kinds of treasures, apparently brought in from exotic locations and cultures. Blankets, rugs and pillows in all the colors of the rainbow, some with strange and peculiar patterns, were draped across tables or hung from large wooden scaffolding. Huge pots and urns made of copper, brass, and even of gold filled tents and stalls, their merchants bargaining with customers.

There were curiosities as well, things Slippy had never seen before but had read about in books and heard of from some other salamanders who had gone travelling. There were globes of the Earth, made out of wood, and brass kaleidoscopes with multicolored crystals; Slippy looked through a few and was

At the marketplace, Slippy met
a strange old salamander selling
clocks. He was dressed in a purple
robe and had a strange moustache
and beard.

amazed at their beauty.

There were wind chimes dangling from posts, making beautiful sounds as the breeze came in off the sea.

A great number of ticking clocks and pocket watches filled one booth where a strange, wizened old salamander, wearing spectacles and a somewhat ludicrous moustache and beard, stood behind boxes of gears, bearings and crystals, keeping his eyes on Slippy as he passed. Slippy smiled and waved, and the old Salamander motioned for Slippy to come near.

The strange old salamander gave Slippy a golden watch. When Slippy looked up to thank him, the salamander was gone!

Cautiously, Slippy approached him ... you can't be too careful. Without saying anything, the old salamander handed him a pocket watch that had a Sun and a Moon etched on its case. When Slippy looked up from the unexpected gift to thank him ... the old salamander was gone!

Feeling slightly unnerved, Slippy placed the timepiece into his travelling bag and continued to follow Sheldon and Mr. Bigsby. In no time his attention, once again, was captured by the hustle and bustle of the marketplace.

Chapter 3: Mr. Lizard's Booth

Slippy had entered a world of fishmongers and food merchants, shouting incoherently above the noise of the crowd. Tables were covered with all different sorts of sea creatures, smelling to high heaven. There were fish of all sizes, shapes and colors, but all more or less recognizable as fish: tuna, flounder, mackerel, swordfish, and even sharks. Any fish you could imagine was lying out on some table, hanging under a tent, or being thrown across the crowd to eager buyers.

Then there were the mollusks, shelled muscles, huge clams, oysters, cuttlefish, nautiluses, octopuses and squids. Looking at all these different creatures, Slippy was no longer surprised that his friend Sheldon would have grown up to be a naturalist.

As they approached the docks, the sea creatures became stranger. Sea horses, sponges, starfish, long-legged crabs and spiny lobsters adorned the tables, and some live specimens were kept in huge tanks. Slippy felt bad for some of the creatures. He imagined how he would feel to be stuck in a tank, with hundreds of people walking by, staring.

Suddenly, Slippy noticed a booth that struck him as strangely familiar and yet very disturbing. It took him a moment to process what he saw ... then he was overcome with anger. It was a lizard (which was not unusual; Slippy had seen a few lizards in the crowd), but this lizard was selling cakes, muffins and other baked goods. His booth had a big sign that said "Mr. Lizard's Cakes and Pastries." The booth and the sign looked brand new, as if they had been set up just that morning.

Slippy became dizzy and somewhat light-headed for a moment; he felt he was about to faint. The lizard was selling the very same pastries he had seen his family and the other salamanders bake just two nights ago. He remembered the purple frosting on the puff cakes. All he could think about was forcing the lizard to eat the whole batch right then and there.

As Slippy made his way through the crowd towards Mr. Lizard's booth to do just that, Sheldon and Mr. Bigsby noticed he was not walking behind them anymore. Looking around, they heard their friend screaming and yelling at the lizard, who was trying very hard to act surprised, as if he had no idea what the salamander was yelling about. A crowd of shoppers had gathered in a circle around the booth, not wanting to get too close to the argument but curious enough to stay and find out what was going on.

When Sheldon saw the lizard's sign and realized what had upset Slippy, he was furious too, but he knew that it was not the time nor place for such a confrontation. Sheldon and Mr. Bigsby grabbed Slippy by the arms and with all their might pulled him away from the booth. They apologized for their friend's odd behavior, even as Slippy continued to shout. Mr. Lizard scowled at all three of them as they disappeared into the crowd.

The Sea Serpent was a large sailing ship anchored off the main pier. A long wooden plank connected the vessel with the dock. At Mr. Bigsby's direction, the three companions walked carefully across the plank onto the ship. Packages and crates were strewn all over the deck as the crew packed goods into crates, tied down barrels, and prepared to set sail.

They could not see Sheldon's father anywhere on deck. Mr. Bigsby said to Sheldon, "Look around for your father, but be

Slippy found a booth where a lizard sold cakes and treats. He saw that they were from the Salamander Village Bakery! Slippy got mad but Sheldon and Mr. Bigsby dragged him away to the Sea Serpent.

sure you're back on the dock by 11:00 o'clock. This ship sets sail at 11:15 o'clock.*"

Slippy thought how unlikely it was that he should have received a free pocket watch just that morning, and he checked the time, just to be safe. It was 10:35 o'clock. Sheldon and

* Salamanders and other animals always say "o'clock," unlike us humans, who only use the phrase on the hour marks.

While they looked around the Sea
Serpent for Sheldon's father, Slippy
climbed down into the storage hold.
It was dark down in the hold, and he
tripped over some rope. He knocked
himself out again, and did not hear
when his friends called for him.

Mr. Bigsby had started asking the crew about Mr. Schumacher's whereabouts when Slippy saw a wooden ladder
descending into the ship and thought he might climb down,
just to take a little peek.

Slippy was on his way into the belly of the ship, looking for Sheldon's father. He was unfamiliar with sailing vessels and didn't realize the hold, as it was called, would be filled with packages, ropes, sacks of food, and other things that don't provide a good surface to walk on.

After a few steps, Slippy lost his footing and tripped on a huge coil of rope, hitting his head on a wooden crate and falling unconscious in the process. The crew came down to look for him, but when nobody responded to their calls, they told Sheldon and Mr. Bigsby that Slippy must have already left the boat.

Chapter 4: The Stowaway

Slippy woke up with a splash of salty water in his face. Three full days after they had set sail, the crew of the Sea Serpent had discovered him, still knocked out and partly covered with ropes.

The Sea Serpent's crew was made up mostly of rodents: mice, a few chipmunks, and Captain Crab-Apple, a sea wizened squirrel from the Western Isles. Several crew members, along with the captain, stood around Slippy, with unpleasant looks on their faces.

"'Peers we have ourselves a stowaway!" said Captain Crab-Apple, in a seaman's accent.

The others nodded in approval, saying things like, "Aye Captain!" and "Argh!" and "What'll we do with 'eem?"

Slippy tried to explain that it was an accident, that he hadn't intended to stay on the ship.

Captain Crab-Apple waved his explanation aside and said, "Excuses! Excuses! You're another mouth to feed, so you'll have to work to earn your keeps, and that means swabbin' the deck!"

"But ...!" began Slippy.

"No buts!" shouted Captain Crab-Apple. "Nothing you tell me is going to change the fact that this is my ship! And on my ship, I make the rules! And the rules is* that everybody does his share! But first, you'll have to learn the jargon!"

Slippy had no idea what jargon** meant. He thought it must be some special word that only sailors understood.

To "teach him the ropes," Captain Crap-Apple introduced him to one of his crew members, a mouse named Squeeks.

Squeeks sat with Slippy for a long while, explaining the various parts of the ship and the language, or jargon, that sailors used while onboard.

"I'll start with the 'A's," explained Squeeks.

"Sure," said Slippy.

"Well," began Squeeks, "'Aboard' means to be on, or in a ship; 'Aft' refers to the part of a boat just behind the middle; 'Ahoy' is what we say when we want to call others' attention."

"Oh," interrupted Slippy, "like 'ahoy mates,' I've heard that

* Captain Crab-Apple should have said, "And the rules ARE that everybody does ..."
** Jargon refers to a set of special words/expressions used by a profession, such as sailors.

68

Three days later, Slippy was awakened by Captain Crab-Apple and the crew of the Sea Serpent, which was far out at sea ... Slippy was very far from home.

before!"

"Exactly!" said Squeeks. "But there's more; an 'Anchor' is the large metal thing that we use to keep a ship from floating away; 'Avast' means stop whatever you're doing; 'Aye-aye' is what we say when the captain gives us an order ..."

"Wow!" exclaimed Slippy. "There sure are a lot of 'A's."

Squeeks was a very helpful crew member who taught Slippy about ships. He told Slippy that they would be sailing for a long time ... Slippy was sad, he wanted to go home.

"Yes, I suppose so," offered Squeeks, "but don't worry, we sailors love the letter 'A.' There aren't too many words left. Anyway, where was I ... oh yes, 'Bow' is the front of a ship; 'Bulwark' is the side of a ship, just above the deck."

"What's a deck?" asked Slippy, having trouble keeping track of all the different terms.

"I'm getting there; the 'D's are next," answered Squeeks, "the 'Deck' is the main floor of the ship which we walk on; a 'Fluke' is one of the bent, pointy parts of an anchor that sticks into the sea-floor; as opposed to the 'Shank,' which is the main shaft of the anchor; the 'Helm' is the ship's steering wheel."

"That big wheel thingy I saw up on the ... deck?" asked Slippy.

"That's right!" explained Squeeks. "The captain steers the ship with that. The 'Hold' is the area below deck, where we store our goods, and where some of the sleeping quarters are; the 'Hull' is the main body of a ship, including the bottom, sides and deck, but not the masts, rigging or sails built on top."

Slippy wondered what "masts" and "rigging" were, but kept quiet, assuming that Squeeks would explain soon enough.

"The 'Jib'," continued Squeeks, "is the small triangular sail at the bow of the ship; a 'Mast' is the tall beam which holds the sails; the 'Poop' ... "

Slippy could not help but giggle. Squeeks gave him a hard look and continued, "... the 'Poop' is the enclosed structure you see at the back of the ship."

Slippy furrowed his brow and bit the inside of his cheek to prevent himself from laughing out loud. He nodded seriously and said, "Yes ... I see. There in the back, is it?"

"Quite right," said Squeeks, still giving Slippy a scowl. He proceeded with the last few words. "As you look up at the bow, or front, of the ship, the left side is called 'Port,' and the right side is called 'Starboard.' 'Rigging' is the system of ropes and pulleys we use to raise the sails. The 'Stern' is the back of the ship ... "

"Near the 'Poop?'" inquired Slippy, very happy to have a chance to use his new vocabulary.

Squeeks paused. He nodded slowly and smiled at Slippy, "You're a fast learner!"

The ship was narrow and creaky. There was no place to be alone aboard, and Slippy always had someone pushing by him ... without even an "Excuse me." Slippy was miserable; he never had to work so hard in his life. Captain Crab-Apple had assigned him to "Swabbin'-the-Deck," of which Slippy was soon to learn the meaning.

Waking up early every day to clean and scrub, or "swab," as it were, was not Slippy's idea of a great time. The captain did keep his side of the bargain, though. Slippy was fed three times a day whatever the other crew members were eating, and he got his own cot to sleep on.

He ate his meals on deck, away from the other crew members. They were a bit too rowdy for Slippy, and he liked looking out at the ocean. One time he saw a school of dolphins swimming by. Another time he saw something deep in the water following alongside the ship. He could not make out its shape, but it appeared to be purple, and it seemed to be peering up at him, out of the depths of the sea. The days were long, the sun was hot, and Slippy was lonely. He soon found himself spending most of his free time with Squeeks.

One day, Squeeks told him, "We're heading south to the Java Archipelago where we'll be picking up coffee by the bagful to transport to the Western Isles." Squeeks indicated that they would not be heading back to the mainland for at least another four months. This put Slippy in a near panic.

"Four months!" he cried. "How will I get back to my family?

Squeeks looked concerned, thought for a moment, and said,

Life on the Sea Serpent was hard for Slippy. One night, he saw a purple monster looking up at him from below the water. It was scary.

"I suggest you disembark at Mocha. The captain won't object, he has plenty of crew members, and there are plenty more waiting in the port town, looking for work." He continued, "You could probably hop on the next boat heading back to the mainland and be back within a week and a half."

'A week and a half? That's not so bad,' said Slippy.

Chapter 5: Pirates

Late in the morning of the 6th day of their voyage, Slippy and Squeeks saw another ship on the horizon. They told Captain Crab-Apple right away. The captain had crew members take shifts keeping an eye on the other vessel, worried that it might be pirates, but soon it became too cloudy to tell.

Slippy got excited when he heard "pirates," but Squeeks gave him another one of his hard looks and said, "Whatever you think you know about pirates, it's wrong."

Slippy had heard that pirates could be rowdy, but in all the stories they ended up having a kind, gentle side. "You mean they're not just dirty old sailors?"

"Pirates practice what we call 'piracy*,'" explained Squeeks; "look it up in the dictionary."

That afternoon, Squeeks invited Slippy to join the crew for a party in the mess hall, which was in the poop, and Slippy agreed. He was growing fond of Squeeks, seeing him as someone trustworthy, and finally told him about Salamander Village and what had happened to his family.

Squeeks seemed genuinely concerned and said that, if he'd had the chance, he would have gone back with Slippy to help him. However, the Sea Serpent was his home, and his loyalty was to the crew and to Captain Crab-Apple, who had saved his life when he was just a mouseling.

As Slippy sat with Squeeks, he watched the rest of the crew; he realized they weren't so bad, after all. However, he noticed that they often drank a dark liquid from some of the barrels.

* pi·ra·cy - practice of a pirate; robbery or illegal violence at sea.

While sailing together, Slippy and Squeeks became good friends. One day, they saw another ship on the horizon, following them.

On more than one occasion, a mug of the stuff was thrust at him, and a friendly face suggested he drink some too. When this happened, Squeeks would look directly at Slippy and shake his head slowly as if to indicate it might not be a good idea. It wasn't long before Slippy knew why. His father had told him about drinks which make people act strangely, sometimes even making them sick. It seemed that this was the stuff his father had been talking about.

Later on, the crew members started to become louder and pushier than before. They laughed a lot and made rude jokes about one another. The jokes turned downright nasty, and feelings were hurt. Two fights broke out, one over a chipmunk sitting in a mouse's seat, the other because one mouse had called another mouse a "baby rat."

Slippy and Squeeks did not like the atmosphere of the party and decided to go out on deck to get some fresh air. As they walked along the starboard side of the ship, they continued to discuss Salamander Village.

"Your family," began Squeeks, "don't they want to fight the lizards?"

"Well," said Slippy, "I think so, but they are outnumbered, and we salamanders never really get into fights."

"I'd like to go clobber those lizards," said Squeeks.

"Me too," said Slippy, "but I think we'll need help if we're ever going to have any hope of succeeding."

Just then they heard a loud noise and shouts coming from the other side of the ship. The vessel they had seen earlier was floating alongside. It was, in fact, a pirate ship called "The Rabid Skunk," manned by shrews who, at that very moment, were using grappling hooks to grab onto the bulwark and pull the Sea Serpent closer to their ship. They were boarding!

In no time the shrews were tying up any crewmembers on deck with thick ropes while the rest of the crew was still oblivious to the dangers upon them, being busy in the poop with their party and all.

Slippy saw the pirates' leader as he came aboard the Sea Serpent, a weasel named Captain One-Eyed Wilbur. He looked dirty and worn out, like an old frayed rope. A large leather eye patch covered what had been his right eye. He wore a big black hat with a white skull and crossbones embroidered on the front, and his left leg was gone, replaced by a wooden peg. A vicious snarl was on his face, a snarl shared by the rest of his

The other ship was a pirate ship. That afternoon, the pirates attacked the Sea Serpent. They captured the sailors, and stole the goods. Slippy and Squeeks found a place to hide, so the pirates did not see them.

The pirate ship was called The Rabid Skunk. One-Eyed Wilbur, a very wicked weasel, was its captain. His crew was mostly shrews. They wanted to take everything from the Sea Serpent, even though it did not belong to them ... that's what pirates do!

crew.

By the time the crew of the Sea Serpent realized what was happening to them, it was too late. There was very little fighting, because the shrews were quite ready for battle while the mice and chipmunks had been too busy drinking ... which had seriously affected their ability to respond. Even Captain Crab-Apple gave up without a fight.

Slippy and Squeeks, however, kept their wits about them;

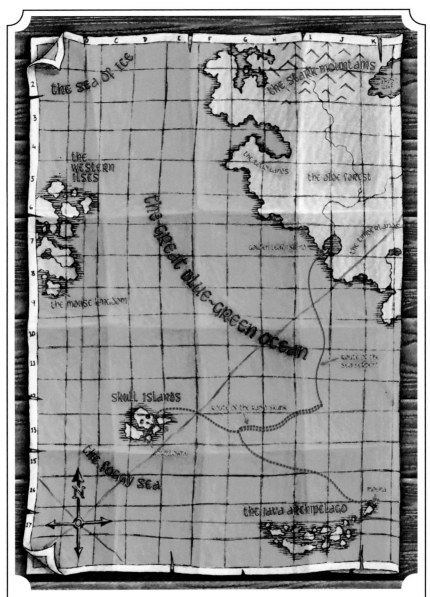

Squeeks's map shows where the Sea
Serpent went, in red; and where the
Rabid Skunk met them, in blue.

they were not planning to be captured by pirates. Realizing that the two of them would not be able to fight them off by themselves, they sneaked below deck and hid behind a barrel, waiting to see what would happen.

The pirates' first task seemed to be cataloguing all the prisoners. They offered any mouse or chipmunk that joined them one half percent of the "loot*," the stolen goods on board. Others who would not join them were offered the option of "walking the plank," right into the depths of the ocean, or to be brought to the Skull Islands and sold as slaves.

One-Eyed-Wilbur said with a grin, "I would never 'force' any of you into slavery! It's your choice!" All the shrews laughed at this, thinking it quite clever.

Many a good mouse, chipmunk and, possibly, one squirrel would go overboard that day if Slippy and Squeeks didn't do anything. Slippy wondered if those thrown overboard might somehow swim to safety, but, remembering the big, purple thing he'd seen, he realized how unlikely that would be. He did not know whom to pity more ... those destined to go overboard or the others who would be sold as slaves. Squeeks was beside himself with anger: he knew he couldn't stop the pirates, but it went against every fiber of his being to just sit and wait.

Finally, Squeeks could not take it anymore. He decided that he'd rather die at the hands of the pirates than stand by and watch what would happen to the crew. He grabbed a short truncheon** and was planning to thwack the heads of a few shrews before they could stop him. He told Slippy to take care of himself, that he should try to stay put until he could get out safely. Slippy, after all, had his own battles to fight and his own family to save from tyranny.

* Loot refers to stolen goods, acquired in a raid.
** A truncheon is a short, thick stick used as a club.

After hiding for a long time, Squeeks wanted to fight the pirates, but Slippy told him to make a plan first. Once the pirates let down their guard, Slippy and Squeeks would make their move.

Slippy was convinced that Squeeks was just trying to make it easier for him. He remembered when Sheldon and Mr. Bigsby had stopped him from confronting Mr. Lizard. He knew that Squeeks would not be able to stop the pirates alone.

So he said, "Wait, Squeeks! I'm going to help you; this is as much my battle as it is yours."

"You are a true friend," said Squeeks. "If we get out of this alive, I will go back to Salamander Village with you. Lizards, beware!"

"Sure thing," said Slippy, "but we're not going to just go out and fight a losing battle. We'll have to come up with a plan to free the crew, hopefully without the pirates even knowing that we're here."

Squeeks was impatient; he wanted to run out, brandishing his club, screaming, "Begone, foul pirates!" But Slippy convinced him to listen.

"Do you want to die bravely ... or win the fight?" he asked.

"I suppose I'd rather win," admitted Squeeks.

They sat down to seriously figure out what to do. With Squeeks's knowledge of the ship and Slippy's determination, they were able to figure out the best way to free the prisoners. Slippy grabbed a long crowbar*, a handy weapon in case things got out of hand; Squeeks had his truncheon. Then the two went out to save the Sea Serpent and her crew.

Chapter 6: The Plan

The first part of their plan was to free Captain Crab-Apple as well as the rest of the mice and chipmunks, none of whom, by the way, had decided to join up with the pirates. Luckily, the shrews thought they had tied everyone up, and their vigilance was down for the moment. Only two shrews were stationed near the base of the ladder, not far from where Slippy and Squeeks had hidden.

Without making a noise, Squeeks and Slippy sneaked up

---

* A crowbar is a long, metal rod, used to pry open crates and barrels.

behind them and clobbered them, knocking them out cold. Quickly, they freed the crew of the Sea Serpent and tied the two guards up with the very rope that had been used to bind Captain Crab-Apple. The Captain thanked them for their heroism and commended them on their strategic thinking skills.

"Waiting until things had quieted down was brilliant," he said. "I might have allowed my anger to cause me to react immediately; your patience has saved us all. Well done, lads! Now let's save this ship!"

Slippy and Squeeks smiled and said, "Aye aye, captain!"

They were not safe yet, though. There were still a couple dozen armed shrews on deck to deal with. They decided to wait until the shrews started carrying the goods over to their ship, since it was better to lose some of the merchandise than the whole ship. They waited and watched to see how the pirates managed the transfer of goods.

They were very organized; certain shrews kept careful notes of what and how much of each item was added to their loot. Captain One-Eyed Wilbur was on his own ship at that moment, which was great news. As shrews were going back and forth between the ships, carrying barrels and crates, the crew counted and waited until only a few of the shrews were left aboard the Sea Serpent.

That was when they made their move: Captain Crab-Apple, Squeeks, Slippy and several other crew members stormed the deck, running straight for the planks. The surprised pirates dropped their crates and barrels; one of them smashed his toes in the process. The mice immediately pushed the planks off into the water, cutting off all access to and from the other

Once the pirates were busy stealing, Squeeks and Slippy rescued Captain Crab-Apple and the rest of the crew. Then they all scared the pirates away together.

boat, while the chipmunks and some of the larger mice surrounded the remaining shrews. As it turned out, only eight shrews were left on board. They didn't even put up a fight, but they did shout really loudly, and it wasn't long before the pirates on the other ship took notice.

Slippy and some of the mice went about removing the grappling hooks; they had more than enough hands for the job. It looked as if they were going to make it.

However, just when Slippy thought they were safe, the grappling hook in his hand was yanked with such a force that it pulled him overboard, and he found himself hanging on for dear life above the sea, being slowly pulled up towards the deck of the Rabid Skunk. With an evil grin on his face, One-Eyed Wilbur himself was hauling up the rope.

That's when he heard Captain Crab-Apple shout out, "Avast!" and, "Let go, Slippy!" He had thought about letting go, but again remembered the big, purple thing lurking below the surface of the water. As he was nearing the top of the bulwark, he heard shouting from the other ship. They were steering back toward the Rabid Skunk; they were going to save him!

The Sea Serpent was side by side with the Rabid Skunk when Slippy heard a voice close by, "Don't worry! We'll get you back!" Looking up, he saw Squeeks reaching out with his hand.

But that's as close as it got, for just then the Rabid Skunk's portholes opened up, and long black cannons emerged from the sides of the pirate ship. They were going to fire on the Sea Serpent! The Sea Serpent did not have cannons, so Captain Crab-Apple ordered his crew to turn to starboard, away from the Rabid Skunk.

Squeeks shouted, "No! Slippy's still over there!" just as Slippy was being lifted onto the deck by a maniacal One-Eyed Wilbur.

"Haar Haar Harr!" he laughed, but his laughter was cut short by a swift club in the gut. Squeeks had jumped over, just in time, and was already taking on three of the shrews. The captain dropped Slippy in order to pull his sword.

The crew of the Sea Serpent fought off the pirates, but Slippy was pulled overboard and wound up on the pirate ship. Squeeks jumped aboard to save him, but they were captured.

Slippy saw the blade swinging toward his friend, and, in a desperate attempt to save Squeeks, he grabbed the captain's arm, seriously doubting by now that there might be a kinder, gentler side to these pirates after all. This fouled up the swing enough for Squeeks to evade being cut in half, but two more shrews were on him before he could do anything else.

Slippy tried in vain to disarm the captain, but he was just too strong. More shrews approached from all sides, and it didn't take long for Slippy to realise that he was beat.

Chapter 7: Down a Hole

The fight was over. The Sea Serpent was far away; only one cannonball had been fired, missing its mark by a wide margin. The pirates had gotten most of the merchandise from the other ship and considered their little venture a success. They had lost ten of their crew members, who would most likely be turned over to the authorities on the Western Isles.

Deep in the hold of the Rabid Skunk, Squeeks and Slippy saw very little of the pirate ship, having been thrown into a prison cell of sorts. It was dark and smelled of foul things. They were only given dried bread to eat and warm water to drink. When Slippy expressed surprise that they were being fed at all, a guard responded that the captain had "special plans" for the two of them.

Several days of this passed, during which very little was said. When they heard the shouts above of "Ahoy, ahoy!" and "Land Ho!" they were almost relieved. However, their relief did not last long.

They were immediately brought before One-Eyed Wilbur, who told them with that well-known snarl on his face: "We're approaching The Skull Islands. You'll be dealt with when we land."

Once they had landed, they were chained together and taken ashore. Slippy saw that the islands were muddy and held very little plant life. Each island was littered by a pile of huge white boulders, some of which looked like the skulls of giant animals. "The Skull Islands" was certainly an appropriate name for the place, but they would not see much of it. They were pushed through a crowd of unsavory looking creatures,

Slippy and Squeeks were taken to
Wormtowne, the pirates' hideout on
The Skull Islands. It was a dangerous
place, and Slippy was afraid.

mostly rats and lizards, probably all pirates of one sort or another.

There were low, dirty looking buildings with tons of stuff stacked up inside, most likely stolen goods. It was almost like the market on Golden Leaf Island, but dirtier and more unfriendly. There were old war ships and beaten-up boats anchored around the harbor; many mean, tough looking shrews, lizards and the occasional mouse were going to and fro on pirate business.

The place was called Wormtowne, the pirates' hideout on the islands. After joing up with two suspicious looking lizards, Captain Wilbur said, "Your punishment is the same as it has been for anyone who fights against us and interferes with our work!"

Apparently, fouling up an act of piracy was a capital crime in pirate law...

Before long, they were heading up a gradual incline, up towards the white boulders ... or bones, as they appeared to be. Huge, empty eye sockets stared at them as they went up along the jagged path. At the top, a few more low buildings surrounded a large, bare patch of ground. In the center of the clearing was a hole, dug straight into the Earth.

"That's where you'll both be going ... The Hole," laughed Captain Wilbur.

"The Hole?" asked Slippy.

"That's right!" said One-Eyed Wilbur. "The Hole: no one's ever made it out alive."

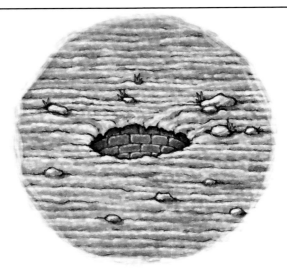

The pirates took Slippy and Squeeks to the middle of the island. In the center of a field was a deep hole, going straight into the Earth.

"Is that so?" responded Squeeks, trying to maintain his dignity.

"That it is," answered Wilbur, "because even if they survive the fall, the dragons get 'em. Are ya havin' any last requests?"

The others around the captain, which included the two lizards and a nasty looking shrew, laughed at this.

"Please," said Squeeks, "could you unchain us?" Slippy and Squeeks were still chained together, and Squeeks figured that it would be better, whatever they would face down in that dark hole, to have the use of their arms and hands unhindered.

"Sure," said Wilbur, "if that's your last request, who am I to deny it?" He looked at Slippy, "And you?"

Slippy answered, "I'd like my bag, please."

While one lizard released their shackles, another handed Slippy his bag. As soon as their hands were free, Squeeks shouted, "You'll pay for what you've done!" running full speed into one of the lizards.

The lizard was caught off guard and went to the ground at the mouse's attack, but One-Eyed Wilbur was there in a heartbeat. He scooped up Squeeks and Slippy and dangled them over The Hole. "Bye bye!" he said sarcastically, as he let them go.

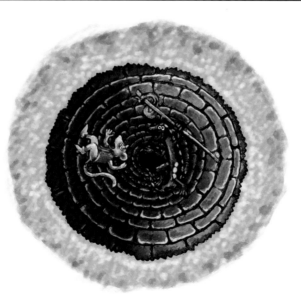

To punish Slippy and Squeeks, One-Eyed Wilbur threw them down "The Hole."

Slippy and Squeeks were stuck in The Hole. Luckily, they were not hurt too badly by the fall. Tomorrow they would find a way out, for sure ... but that's another story.

Falling down was the worst part. Slippy had no idea what they would land on ... a loud crunch answered his question; bones covered the floor around them, other unfortunate victims of pirate "justice," it seemed. Though the bones did not offer a soft landing by any stretch of the imagination, they did provide some cushion from the fall, which left Squeeks and Slippy with only minor bruises and cuts.

They brushed themselves off and looked around their new surroundings. In the dim light that came through The Hole above them, they could barely make out any details. After a while, their eyes adjusted to the darkness, and they were able to see two large passageways leading away into the gloom. Maybe there was hope.

Squeeks, it turned out, had filled his pockets with some of the dried bread from the pirate ship. Along with the contents of Slippy's bag, it made for a reasonable meal, considering the circumstances. Since they seemed to be in no immediate danger and were really too tired and aching to go anywhere, the two companions decided to wait and rest in the cavern for a while. Once they felt better, they would certainly find their way out of this mess.

Little did they know ... but that's another story.

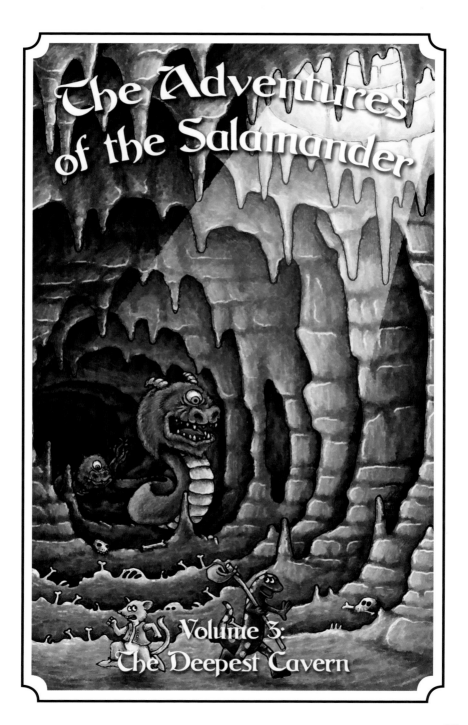

The Adventures of the Salamander

Volume 3:
The Deepest Cavern

THE ADVENTURES OF THE SALAMANDER
by Michael Klaus Schmidt

BOOK I • VOLUME 3

═══════════

The Deepest Cavern

Chapter 1: Two Passages

Slippy let out a deep sigh, "Will this never end?" On his way to find help for his friends and family at Salamander Village, which had been taken over by a bunch of mean-spirited lizards, Slippy had run into one problem after another. The very latest was a rather unpleasant, to say the least, encounter with some pirates. That's why Slippy and his friend Squeeks, the mouse, found themselves at this very moment deep underground on one of The Skull Islands, left for dead by the evil pirate captain One-Eyed Wilbur.

After heroically rescuing the crew of the Sea Serpent, the two companions had been thrown into The Hole! Miraculously, they had survived the fall. Now they were trapped in a cave, surrounded by the bones of previous adversaries of One-Eyed Wilbur and his crew, with a difficult decision to make.

Slippy's eyes had more or less adjusted to the dim light, but Squeeks could barely see his own shoes. However, squeaky mice and slimy salamanders have other senses that they can rely on when they get lost in the dark. After eating, resting and chatting a bit about cheese, they decided to go to each of the passages, to listen to any sounds they could hear and to sniff any smells they could smell in order to help them find a way out.

The first passage smelled of earth and dampness, not altogether unpleasant but not particularly promising, either. They had hoped for, and would have much preferred, some fresh air, or at least a sea breeze wafting through from the surface. In the distance they could hear the echo of water dripping: "plip-plop, plip-plop," as it proceeded to sculpt and carve out the caverns of the Underearth.

"The Underearth?" asked Slippy when Squeeks used the word.

"Yes," replied Squeeks, "where I'm from, that's what we call these caves. They say they go down all the way to the center of the Earth!"

"The Center of the Earth?" Slippy was impressed.

They made their way over to the second passage ... and could

The pirates had thrown Slippy and Squeeks into The Hole. At the bottom they found nothing except bones, a few bugs ... and two dark passages that led to who-knows-where. They had to choose which way to go.

tell well before they got there that this was not going to be their first choice. An odor like that of a barn, only stronger, blasted them with its hot stench. They could hear movement and a heavy breathing noise, punctuated with grunts and snarls. Something big seemed to lurk down the passage; luckily it seemed not to have noticed them ... yet. Slowly and carefully, they tried to sneak back to the first passage, hoping not to alert the monster.

Suddenly, they heard a loud grunt and stood still, frozen with fear. As their hearts pounded, they knew that the creature must have sensed their presence as they snooped around; perhaps it had smelled them. Trying not to make any noise, Slippy and Squeeks stood like statues ... but it was too late!

A huge, dark, sinister shape appeared in the already darkened passage. Two points of green light glowed in the gloom. Slippy assumed they were the creature's eyes, but then the two green points started moving independently of each other. Slippy could not even begin to imagine what the creature might look like.

As the thing approached and slowly entered the main cavern, the light coming through the shaft above illuminated what turned out to be two creatures. Each had a single eye in the middle of its head, a wide mouth with enormous sharp teeth, and a long, serpent-like body. The one in front was considerably larger than the other; it might have been the mom. The creatures were a dark green color with scaly skin, their tails ending in a tangle of long tendrils.

Where these the dragons captain One-Eyed-Wilbur had mentioned? Slippy tried to remember what his friend Sheldon back on Golden Leaf Island had told him about chimeras. Had he been here, Sheldon would, no doubt, have been fascinated.

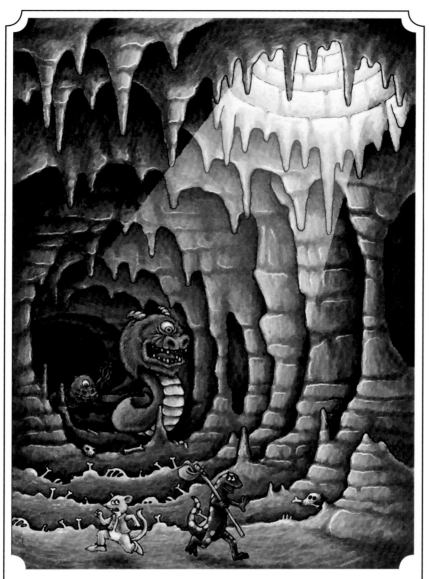

They chose the wrong passage and were chased by two green, one-eyed, scary, cave monsters. They ran for their lives!

He would have had some keen insights as to the creatures' diet or nesting habits ... which, one must admit, would have served little benefit under the current circumstances. The dragons squirmed on the floor, making their way toward their prey ... namely Slippy and Squeeks.

Slippy noticed that the two creatures slowed down, seemingly reluctant to pass into the dim light that shone down through the shaft. Before giving them time to work their way around the light, Slippy and Squeeks realized that they might be able to outrun the things. So they did.

Chapter 2: The Staircase

With surprising speed, Slippy and Squeeks ran back toward the first passage, hoping they would not run into any more of the terrifying creatures. It was a reasonable hope, considering the lack of foul odor and all. As fast as they could, they ran onward, glancing back from time to time. Along the way, their ability to see improved somehow. They found themselves on a continuously downward slope, they hoped that they might approach some sort of exit. When they finally allowed themselves to slow down a bit to survey their surroundings, they noticed a smaller opening at the side of the main passage.

They could still hear a distant grunting noise as it approached from behind, indicating the relentless pursuit of the dragons. Squeeks and Slippy quickly decided to investigate the smaller side passage. They could hear the sound of running water in the distance, and the air was relatively fresh. Due to the passage's small opening, they hoped the two creatures would be unable to chase after them.

The passage appeared to have been carved out of the rock. The edges were roughly squarish, and rectangular bricks had been used to close off certain sections of the wall. The narrow trail turned downward and around, curving backwards from the main passage.

It continued down two flights of stone stairs, and, after about one hundred yards, it opened up into another large cavern. The walls of this cavern were producing some sort of light ... just a faint, green glow. The cavern itself was shaped like a huge, vertical shaft, its ceiling and floor too far away to see.

They could see that a stairway had been built around the circumference of the shaft; it descended downwards into the pit in a spiral.

The stairs were made of what appeared to be spare parts, pieces of rusty metal, bolted to boards, and planks of old wood. Rope was used to tie some parts of the staircase to others and to secure them to the walls of the cavern. Water dripped and dropped here and there, along the walls of the chamber. They could see narrow streams heading, as if with a purpose, into the darkness below. Steam issued from somewhere deep beneath, right up the center of the cavern, keeping the place damp. The cool, moist air was not altogether unpleasant, and Slippy thought it felt good against his sensitive amphibian skin.

Slowly and hesitantly, they descended the wet, creaking staircase. After a long period of quiet, Squeeks asked Slippy about his village.

"It's a wonderful place, you know," said Slippy, "I grew up there, lived there my whole life."

Luckily, the other passage did not have any monsters. It led them to a deep shaft with a crazy stairway going all the way down.

Squeeks said, "What about the lizards; what do they want?"

"They want our cakes," Slippy answered. He told Squeeks about Mr. Lizard's booth at the marketplace on Golden Leaf Island.

"So that's their game, is it?" squeaked Squeeks. "Enslaving your family and taking credit for the pastries, cakes and muffins? That's downright miserable!"

"Yes," agreed Slippy, "I'm the only chance my family has, and somehow I've botched it up and wound up down here, climbing into what appears to be the center of the Earth!"

They heard a hissing sound, and, shortly thereafter, another blast of steam issued forth from below.

"Don't worry," said Squeeks, "we're far from the center of the Earth. We're deep for sure, but not that deep."

Somehow that didn't improve Slippy's nagging suspicion that he was heading in exactly the wrong direction.

"What about you?" he asked Squeeks. "Where do you come from, and how did you wind up with Captain Crab-Apple?"

"Oh, that's a story," answered Squeeks, as he adopted a rather important tone. "It all started when I was a little mouseling. I was going to the Great Cheese Festival with my family, down by the Mouse King's Cheese Castle on the Western Isles where I grew up."

"Mmmm, cheese!" said Slippy.

"Anyway," continued Squeeks, "our family had a huge wheel

The stairway seemed to go on forever. They had no choice but to find out what was at the bottom. On the way down, Slippy told Squeeks all about Salamander Village and the trouble with the lizards.

of Double Gloucester (Cheese names are considered proper nouns in Mouse), and we were rolling it to sell at the festival."

"I always wondered why they made cheese into wheels," commented Slippy.

"Of course," replied Squeeks, "we mice had a lot to do with that*. Anyway, my Dad was rolling the Double Gloucester up a hill. He told me to stay behind with my mother and my big sister Emma until the wheel was safely over the crest; he said it was too dangerous for a little mouse like me. Then my

* Who knows, cheese wheels have been around for thousands of years, as have mice!

mom went off the trail for a moment to gather some flowers, and Emma went along with her. I ended up on the trail all by myself."

As they descended, Slippy could hear the sound of machinery as something chugged along in the depths of the Earth. He couldn't imagine what it might be, all the way down there, or why someone would keep such a machine running.

Coming back to their conversation, Slippy asked, "They didn't

Then Squeeks told Slippy the story about his name. When he was a young mouseling, Squeeks was helping his dad roll a big wheel of cheese to the cheese festival.

Squeeks stayed with his mom and sister, while his father rolled the big cheese wheel up a hill. The wheel slipped and came rolling down the hill, right at Squeeks!

go too far, though, your mom and Emma?"

"No, I could still see them through the bushes, so I wasn't worried or anything. That's the first time I saw Captain Crab-Apple; he was coming up the road from behind us. He started waving at me, and, being friendly, I waved back.

"Then I heard it ... like rolling thunder. I turned to see the cheese wheel coming down the hill, right towards me. When

I was little, if I got scared I used to squeak real loud and roll myself into a ball. That's how I got the name "Squeeks."

"Anyway, that's just what I did. I thought I was about to be squashified, flattened, pulverated ... I never even understood how it missed me.

"My parents told me about it later, about how Captain Crab-Apple ran and picked me up, rolling with me to the side of the road ... just as the Double Gloucester was about to flatten us both. They were so grateful to the Captain after that; he had saved my life. They invited him over many times, and we all became great friends."

There were lights below them now, real lights, like those from an oil lamp. Sure enough, when Slippy looked down, he could make out the top of what seemed to be a large chimney spewing out steam at the bottom of the shaft. Along the edges of the cavern, small sconces had been attached to the walls. Only a few of the lamps were lit, but they helped make navigating the stairs much easier.

Squeeks continued, "When I grew old enough, I asked my parents if I could join the crew of the Sea Serpent, and they were very happy to hear me say that. They said 'yes' right away."

"And you've been at it ever since," added Slippy.

"Yep," said Squeeks with a hint of nostalgia, "we always went back home to visit my folks, every time we stopped at the Mouse Kingdom. Lots of sailors never get to see their families; they're always stuck on the boat, afraid to lose their jobs if they disembark*. Not so with Captain Crab-Apple; he always insisted his crew go home when they had the chance. He said

* Disembark: To leave a ship, aircraft or other vehicle.

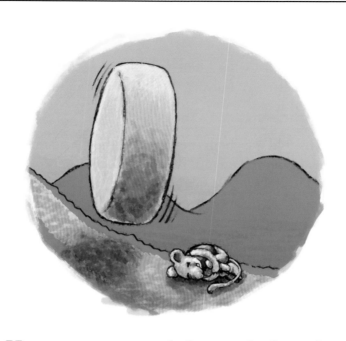

He was so scared, he curled up into a little ball, making a cute little squeaking noise, until Captain Crab-Apple saved him. Ever since, people have called him "Squeeks."

it keeps the crew happy and loyal, and he was right. He's hard as nails, Crab-Apple, but he's a straight shooter."

Chapter 3: The City of the Troglodytes

The huge machine continued to rumble about 200 feet below on what seemed to be the bottom of the cavern. There was movement down there; small lights seemed to be heading this way and that. The stairs ended abruptly then, leading into another opening in the wall. A passage took them down another set of stairs, carved into the rock and worn with great age and use. More sconces lined the walls of the passage, and it was much brighter than in the main shaft.

As the passage curved around, they found themselves emerging high up on the ceiling of what seemed to be a huge circular cavern. The stairs continued down, once again built out of metal, wood and ropes. The last 100 feet or so became a bit worrisome for Slippy and Squeeks; they saw a lot of activity down below. It seemed that the creatures, which had lights fixed to their heads, had spotted them and started to alert the rest of the city ... for that's what it was.

Buildings had been erected on the bottom of the cavern, amid huge stalagmites* that decorated the chamber. There was a lake right in the middle, from which a river issued forth, travelling through the center of the town and out through another large opening where it disappeared into darkness.

Right in the middle of the lake, the machine they had heard sat on huge stilts made of metal and wood. It seemed to be an engine of some sort, its furnace being fed with coal by several workers. Great wheels and gears rotated endlessly, and steam issued forth from the pipes at the top of the device. The framework of the huge appliance was constructed of great rusted sheets of metal, bolted together to house the burner and other inner workings.

Tubes extended down into the lake, where water was extracted to be heated into the steam that was used to power the great wheels. The gears turned other smaller gears, which in turn powered other, even smaller ones that turned long axles.

---

* Stalagmites are deposits of calcium carbonate, formed by trickling of water, and rising up from the floor of a cave.

When they finally reached the bottom,
they found a huge cavern with an
amazing underground city. Right in the
middle was ...

... a great big steam engine. Strange creatures lived in the city and ran the engine. They had come to the City of the Troglodytes.

These axles extended out into different parts of the city and out into the walls of the cavern, their purpose being hidden from Slippy, who was not at all familiar with modern contrivances of this nature.

Off to the sides of the cavern, Slippy noticed more openings that had been carved into the walls. Tracks led down to the passages and out into the darkness. Small carts were moving back and forth on the tracks, some linked together in a chain. Chunks of black stone filled many of the carts, and more of the strange, pale creatures could be seen pushing the carts and emptying their contents into the great furnace, which provided the heat necessary to run the steam engine.

As they stepped off the final flight of stairs onto the cavern floor, they were greeted by the oddest assortment of creatures either Slippy or Squeeks had ever encountered. They were friendly enough and, though surprised by the arrival of the two companions, did not seem to be threatened at all by them.

The inhabitants of this subterranean city were very unusual. They were about Slippy's height, with large round eyes, stooped shoulders, and tails. Their skin was pale and somewhat shiny; many of them wore metal helmets with lights attached to the top. Slippy could not tell what kind of creatures they were and truly wished Sheldon had been there. Two of the creatures walked up to Slippy and Squeeks, very graciously extended their hands in greeting and said, "Greetings! Welcome to the City of Troglodytes."

Slippy and Squeeks shook hands for a while, as many of the strange creatures seemed very eager to meet them. Finally, Squeeks asked, "What is this place?"

"We live here," one of the two troglodytes replied. "My name

When Slippy and Squeeks reached
the bottom, they were greeted by
strange creatures, the troglodytes,
who were busy pushing wheelbarrows
filled with coal.

is Torgle; I'm the mayor of the city, and you two are the first
visitors we've had in over twenty years!"

"Wow," replied an amazed Slippy.

"We'd like to have a party in your honor," said Mayor Torgle,
"we insist."

"Why, thank you," said Squeeks, "but we really need to find

our way back up to the surface as soon as possible."

"The surface?" asked one of the other troglodytes. "That's no problem; you can take the elevator."

All the troglodytes nodded in approval. "But you'll need to get to the Earth's core first; that's where the elevator room is," one of them added.

Slippy and Squeeks were, understandably, a bit skeptical and hesitantly asked, "There's an elevator at the center of the Earth?"

"There are several!" said Torgle. "We've built all sorts of different things down here. Have you noticed our steam engine?" he inquired as he pointed to the huge machine in the center of the cavern. "It powers the whole town, heats the chambers and runs our mining equipment."

The troglodytes were very industrious, it seemed. "Tell you what," said Torgle, "you let us have a party for you, and we'll assign you a guide to lead you to the elevators. We won't take long; don't worry, you probably need to rest and freshen up a bit after your long journey, anyway, right?"

"I suppose so," conceded Slippy, his feet aching from all the running and climbing.

"Tonight after the party, you can rest here in the city, and then first thing in the morning you can head out for the elevators."

"Sounds like a plan," agreed Squeeks. "How long will it take us to reach these elevators?"

"Oh, that shouldn't take more than a few hours on the tracks."

Torgle was Mayor of the city. He was happy to have Squeeks and Slippy as guests. He told them they could get back to the surface by taking a mining cart to the elevator room. But first they would have a party!

The troglodytes began to disperse and prepare for the party. Slippy could see them start up great cooking fires and haul out baskets of food and drink. Tables were set up and covered with bright colored paper; streamers were hung, and the place began to look more and more festive by the minute.

Soon, everyone was asked to take their seats. Mayor Torgle made a speech about their "two honored guests," and how "great an occasion" it was that they had arrived. After their

The Troglodytes never had guests, so they threw a party in honor of Slippy and Squeeks. The party was great fun, but they were tired and needed rest.

abuse at the hands of the pirates, Slippy and Squeeks were quite pleased to receive such exemplary treatment.

Plates were placed in front of them, and huge platters of food were placed on each table. Cave cricket soup and roasted pill bug were the main courses. They also had something called fish-sticks, made with breaded fish meat, as a side dish. Slippy had never tasted anything so wonderful, unless you count Mrs. Bristlebottom's roasted slug.

One troglodyte commented on how their kids would eat the

live cave fish raw. It seemed like a strange comment, but then Slippy remembered that, when he was still in his larval stage, he would eat live fish in Salamander Pond all the time.

Chapter 4: The Earth-Wyrms

The party was wonderful, well worth the time it took to set it up. Slippy was truly grateful for the troglodytes' hospitality. He felt, in a strange way, as if he was home, that the troglodytes were like his own family. It then occurred to him that the City of the Troglodytes was a lot like Salamander Village, particularly the lake ... like Salamander Pond.

He realized that there were no baby troglodytes anywhere to be seen in the city, just like Salamander Village. Salamanders were amphibians, born in the water and breathing water like fish. Only when they grow up do they acquire lungs with which to breath air. It occurred to him that the troglodytes might very well be amphibians, too! Slippy was determined to find out. But first he needed to rest.

He and Squeeks were led to one of the buildings to stay with a troglodyte family. Their hosts, Dorgo Wellbelow and his wife Madge, brought a few blankets and some slippers for Slippy and Squeeks. They showed them their rooms, which were small and cozy. Each had a comfy bed and a small table with a candle. After a few pleasantries, Slippy prepared to sleep and blew out the candle.

"Oh, we don't turn those lights off, ever," asserted Madge as she re-lit the candle; "the light keeps the earth-wyrms away."

"Earth-worms?" asked Slippy.

Slippy and Squeeks stayed with a troglodyte family. They learned all about the dangerous creatures they had seen earlier, which were called earth-wyrms.

"No, earth-wyrms, as in earth-dragons," replied Madge.

Slippy immediately knew what she was referring to. "We saw them on the way down! Huge green creatures with big teeth and one eye ...," he hesitated, as he realized he had almost forgotten the whole encounter, being tired and all.

"That's them," said Madge, "they hate the light, won't come

near it."

"That's good to know," said Slippy, understanding why the creatures had been hesitant to cross through the beam of light. "Are they dangerous?"

"Oh my, yes!" said Madge with a smile. "They've gobbled up whole villages of us trogs in the past, always at night, when everyone's asleep and the lights are out. That's why we no longer turn off the lights."

Earth-wyrms were known to eat whole cities of troglodytes. However, they can't stand light, so Slippy kept his candle lit.

On that note, Slippy bid the trogs a pleasant evening and attempted to get some sleep. Slippy dreamed of dark passageways and strange noises all night long, but each time the dream started to get at all scary, he remembered that he had a light on his head. When he turned on the light, he could again see his friends, and the darkness would go away.

When he woke, he felt refreshed ... and a bit perplexed. Strange dream, why would he have a light on his head? He shrugged it off and made his way downstairs to see if there was anything to eat. Sure enough, Dorgo and Madge were up and busy as they prepared breakfast. Squeeks was already awake; he sat in a lounge chair as he sipped his morning juice.

Slippy observed as Dorgo scrambled some fish eggs with the strangest device he had ever seen. It was like one of the hand-held egg beaters he'd used back home, but it had an unlikely number of huge gears and whirling parts. The device was connected to a socket in the wall, which rotated endlessly. When he looked out the window, he saw that the socket was powered by one of the axles that came from the great troglodyte engine. He began to see the wisdom behind these creatures' somewhat odd behavior.

After breakfast, Slippy and Squeeks were escorted to one of the many mining tracks which led out of the city. Mayor Torgle was there, along with a few other troglodytes.

"So this will be goodbye, for now," said the mayor. "As you can see, we've already prepared for your journey."

The mayor indicated the set of mine carts that had been filled with some provisions, blankets, food and three mining helmets, equipped with lamps. A young troglodyte stood ready, prepared to travel along with them.

The next day, Slippy and Squeeks
met Diggy. Diggy was the troglodyte
who would lead them to the elevator
room, where they could get back to
the surface.

"This is Diggy," said Mayor Torgle, "he's one of our best min-
ers and is very familiar with this stretch of track. It should
take you directly to the planet's core."

Diggy extended his hand, and Slippy shook it heartily, being
very pleased to have a guide along for the ride.

Squeeks expressed his warmest thanks to the mayor and the other trogs, and then hopped into one of the carts.

The mayor nodded and said, "You'd best be going, because if you take too long to say goodbye, it becomes awkward for everyone."

After Slippy and Diggy loaded themselves aboard the carts, Diggy took the controls, which consisted of a long stick.

"The stick," Diggy explained, "is simply a breaking mechanism; when it's released, the cart moves by gravity down the track."

Diggy continued, "In order to return, we use a series of chains powered by the generator, which pull the carts back up." He pointed upwards, and Slippy saw the mechanism above the track, bolted to the ceiling of the passage.

"Goodbye!" shouted Mayor Torgle and some of the other trogs.

Slippy and Squeeks waved back at them as the cart moved along, slowly at first, but then faster and faster until it felt almost dangerous to the visitors.

Chapter 5: The Center of the Earth

They travelled for a while in silence until Slippy thought he'd ask Diggy about the troglodytes. "I didn't see any children in the city," he said, "are they away somewhere?"

"No," said Diggy, "trog children live in the water."

Slippy had been right. "You're amphibians too!" he announced enthusiastically. "We salamanders are also amphibians; I thought you guys seemed familiar."

Diggy looked at him as if for the first time; the resemblance was obvious now. "Well, I'll be a tadpole's uncle!" he cried joyfully.

The two talked about their childhoods, growing up in ponds and such. Slippy informed Diggy about the plight of the Salamanders in his home village. Squeeks added a few observations of his own, and the three of them bonded as they travelled, just a bit too fast, down the well-lit passages.

Sometimes the passage would open up into huge caverns where strong columns held the tracks in place. One of these caverns contained buildings, much like those in the City of the Troglodytes. Diggy said the residents of Trogtown, as he called it, were all trogs, as well. They had engines similar to the one back home.

It was amazing for Slippy to see such an advanced civilization under the surface of the Earth. He would have never guessed there were any intelligent creatures living this far underground, and here he was ... their long lost relative. He wondered if his own family's origins were from somewhere under the Earth, as well.

"Do you trogs ever get up to the surface?" he asked Diggy.

"Sure," Diggy responded, "once in a while. But never for very long."

Suddenly, the passage ahead grew brighter and brighter, and the temperature went up considerably. Diggy turned around and said, "Don't worry; it's just the 'Lake of Fire.'"

Sure enough, the passage opened into a large cave, the floor of which was apparently made of fire. "These are the Magma Chambers, and that's molten rock down there," explained Diggy, "very hot stuff, indeed! Our engineers are presently trying to figure out how to utilize the heat energy for our machinery and engines."

Slippy could feel the heat as it emanated from below. Before it became too unbearable, they were back into another passageway, rattling along as if nothing had happened.

A while later, they encountered another huge cavern, unlit, except along the tracks. Far below, Slippy saw huge dark green shapes as they squirmed about between the stalagmites. Taking a sharp breath, he whispered, "Earth-wyrms."

"Yep," answered Diggy, "there's no shortage of those down here."

They seemed almost peaceful from a safe distance, just living their lives down below, but after what Madge had told him, he shuddered to think about meeting one face to face again.

Suddenly, the cart began to rapidly slow down. Diggy pulled the brake lever with all his might. Looking ahead, Slippy saw that the track had a gap where something seemed to have broken through the supports. They stopped several yards from the edge of a deep drop. A huge stalactite* lay at the bottom of the cavern; it must have become dislodged from the ceiling somehow.

A single ladder led down to the base of the tracks. They gathered up as much as they could carry and proceeded to de-

* Stalactites, in contrast to stalagmites, extend down from the ceiling of a cave. They too consist of deposits of calcium carbonate, formed by trickling water.

Diggy guided Slippy and Squeeks along the mining tracks, to the center of the Earth. They went through many strange caverns, and over the "Lake of Fire," a magma chamber where it was very, very hot.

On their journey, Slippy and Diggy discovered that troglodytes and salamanders were both amphibians, born with gills to breathe water, and taking to land only when they get older.

scend down the ladder, Diggy first. He didn't seem worried, so Slippy and Squeeks tried not to be worried, either. It was not easily done, and the farther they climbed down, the more Slippy thought about the earth-wyrms gobbling up villages of troglodytes.

"Shouldn't we head back?" he asked, his voice tinged with fear.

"No, this is the only way to the elevators," said Diggy. "Don't worry; I've done this before. When I get back to town, I'll let them know, and a team will be sent out to repair the tracks."

As they climbed down the ladder, they could hear the muffled squirming of the earth-wyrms below them. The ladder creaked with some unusually loud noises; perhaps the three of them were too heavy for it. The answer to this question became all too apparent when Slippy and his two companions fell, the ladder having snapped under their combined weight.

The floor was made largely of a soft, sand-like material, and, fortunately, no one hurt themselves too badly in the fall. However, it was very dark at the bottom of the cavern.

Diggy explained calmly, "We're not far from the elevator chamber; we just need to climb up the next ladder and get back onto the tracks; from there we can walk the rest of the way ... oh, no!"

The way Diggy said these last words made Slippy's heart sink; "What's wrong?"

"My helmet! I've lost my helmet!" cried Diggy.

To Slippy this seemed like the least of their problems; he still had his helmet strapped on, but he hadn't needed it, yet.

In one cavern the tracks had been damaged, so they had to climb down a ladder. Oops, the ladder broke, and they fell to the ground!

There were no falling rocks, so he couldn't quite figure out why Diggy was so upset. Suddenly, the squirming sound of the earth-wyrms became louder as they closed in on the three travellers. Small green points of light could be seen in the darkness around them; they were completely surrounded!

"Mine's gone, too!" said Squeeks, his voice in a panic.

While Slippy felt kind of lucky to still have his helmet, he did not understand why it was so important to his friends. The

At the bottom of the dark cavern, Slippy and his friends were surrounded by hungry earth-wyrms. They were doomed!

sound of labored breathing around them, however, worried him greatly, especially when he started to feel the hot breath of the earth-wyrms.

Without knowing why, Slippy reached up and felt around on his helmet. The breathing became louder; the stench of the creatures was unbearable; huge black shapes loomed all around in the darkness. Slippy felt something on the helmet ... a switch! Suddenly, it all made sense that Diggy and Squeeks missed their helmets so much. "We're all gonna die!" lamented Diggy.

"Not today!" announced Slippy triumphantly. As he flipped
the switch on his helmet, light flooded the cavern, like the
sun after a rainstorm. The huge creatures were just a few feet
away, but they jerked and writhed in pain. The light produced
by the helmet was too much for the earth-wyrms, and they
squirmed away as quickly as they could in all directions.

Slippy realized that his strange dream had come true: the darkness, the light on his head, his friends safe and sound ... it was
all there.

Just then, Slippy remembered that the
helmet he was wearing had a light
switch. With one "click," Slippy sent
the earth-wyrms squirming away.

They quickly picked up whatever provisions they could find. As they plodded through the sandy bottom of the cavern, Slippy told his friends about the dream, and they both nodded and voiced their approval.

"My mom used to have dreams that came true," said Squeeks; "she would tell us all in the morning what she had dreamt, and, at some point during the day, it would happen. We would all be amazed. Not every day, mind you, but enough to make you wonder."

"Wow!" said Diggy. "That's impressive; your mom must be a special lady."

"She sure is, and not just because of her dreams, either," he answered proudly.

The rest of their journey was fairly uneventful. Slippy was glad for this, because any more events might have spelled disaster for the travellers. They climbed back up to the tracks and began walking; a platform ran along the length of the track, so movement was easy. The passageways were well lit, and that meant no more threat from the earth-wyrms. After they stopped for a brief lunch, the three friends continued at a good pace until they reached their destination.

"Here we are," Diggy said finally, "the elevator chamber!"

Before them was an amazing sight, a huge spherical chamber with holes and shafts that led off in every direction. A series of metal and wooden platforms had been built around the edges of the chamber, all attached to the outer walls. The center of gravity of this room was in its empty center. It was the center of the Earth!

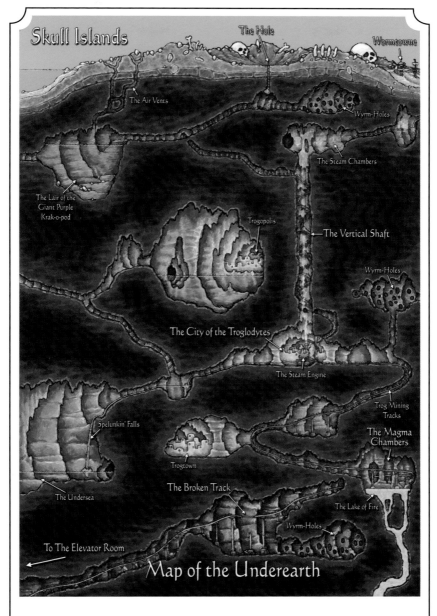

Skull Islands

The Hole

Wormtowne

The Air Vents

Wyrm-Holes

The Steam Chambers

The Lair of the
Giant Purple
Krak-o-pod

Trogopolis

The Vertical Shaft

Wyrm-Holes

The City of the Troglodytes

The Steam Engine

Trog Mining
Tracks

Spelunkin' Falls

The Magma
Chambers

Trogtown

The Undersea

The Broken Track

The Lake of Fire

Wyrm-Holes

To The Elevator Room

Map of the Underearth

The path taken by Slippy and Squeeks
through the "Underearth."

Once they escaped the earth-wyrms, they had no trouble getting to the elevator room, which was in the center of the Earth! From there, elevators led to all different places on the Earth's surface.

The platforms led to a few dozen huge shafts that had been carved into the rock. Noisy geared mechanisms powered numerous elevators, made of old, rusty metal and aged wood, zipping up and down the shafts. The entire chamber vibrated as the gears turned and squeaked. Troglodytes hustled and bustled throughout the chamber and stood by some of the elevators as they repaired broken gears and pulleys; they looked as if they knew what they were doing.

Chapter 6: The Old Rusty Elevator

An old trog approached them with a broad smile on his face. "Diggy, my boy!" he shouted over the noise of the machines.

"Hey, Grandpa," replied Diggy.

They all introduced themselves at that point, firm handshakes were exchanged, and it was an altogether pleasant experience.

"How can I help you boys?" Grandpa asked.

Diggy answered, "These two need to get to the surface."

"Well, you've come to the right place!" said Grandpa firmly. "Where would you like to go?"

Slippy said, "I really need to get to the Olde Forest."

"Okay," said Grandpa, pulling out a map, "then I think your best bet will be with the Stark Mountain Express. From there it's just a few days' journey through the mountains and another day and a half down the Clearmountain Stream to the Olde Forest."

Slippy looked at the map in Grandpa's hands and found the Olde Forest near the center. Sure enough, a small label northwest of the forest marked a spot in the Stark Mountains, which indicated an elevator shaft. Slippy was surprised to see Salamander Village on the map. Then he noticed another elevator shaft, even closer to the Olde Forest, to the east.

"What's this one?" he asked.

Grandpa laughed, "Oh, you don't want to go there. That's right in the heart of the Dry Lands. No place for us amphibians!" Grandpa had seen the connection between the trogs and Slippy right away.

A loud noise alerted Slippy to the fact that an elevator had just arrived somewhere in the chamber. He looked up to see a group of birds exiting one elevator and beginning to board another. A trog stood by and helped the birds, as he made sure they got on the right one.

"Migration route," explained Grandpa, "they've been doing this for the last three winter seasons. We've had some pretty important birds come through, bird dignitaries, entertainers and the like."

"Wow," said Slippy, "I've never met a bird."

"Oh, they're okay," said Grandpa, "like other folks I guess. Some of them are really great!"

"And others?" asked Slippy, wondering what the birds who were not great might be like.

"Oh, I don't like to make blanket statements about anyone," said Grandpa, "It's easy to try to generalize, because they're so

Diggy's grandfather, 'Grandpa,' worked in the elevator room. He helped Slippy find the best elevator to take him back home. Grandpa knew all about the elevators.

different, you know, with the wings and feathers and all. But birds are just as likely to be as good or bad as anyone else we meet."

Slippy thought about this, and wondered whether the lizards who invaded his village were as likely to be as good or bad as the average salamander.

Diggy and Grandpa decided to come along on the elevator, just for the ride up ... but that's another story.

Grandpa led them around the chamber to an elevator door that stood open. A sign above it read "Stark Mountain Express." The sign on another elevator next to it said "Stark Mountain Standard."

"The standard elevators have stops along the way," explained Diggy. "They stop at different cities and caverns of interest, for tourists and such."

"Amazing," said Slippy, "I never knew any of this was down here."

As Slippy and Squeeks boarded the elevator, Grandpa and Diggy surprised them when they stepped aboard with them.

"We're coming with," said Grandpa, "just for the ride up!"

"Great!" said Slippy, as the elevator jerked to life and proceeded its steady, if somewhat squeaky, course to the surface. He was thinking about how great it was that he would finally be on the surface again, able to get home to Salamander Village.

Little did he know ... but that's another story.

Appendix I: The Original Tale

On the left is the original "Adventures of the Salamander," which I wrote when I was 5 years old. Actually, my mom typed it, but the story behind it and the illustrations were all mine.

Do you recognize any of the creatures I drew? In the first part, the lizards invade Salamander Village, armed with lasers and lizard-shaped flying machines. Slippy, armed with a mounted laser cannon of sorts, gives up the fight and runs away, swimming behind a rock.

In part two, the earth-wyrms appear, in all their horrifying green-ness. Slippy once again runs away and hides behind another rock! Surely, Slippy was a great strategist!

However, a spider, which you have not met in the new volumes, yet, is waiting for him there. The spider is obviously bigger than Slippy and could easily devour him. This time, fate is on Slippy's side. The Spider is squeamish and runs away from Slippy because of his slimy skin.

Finally, part four concludes the adventure when Slippy ventures underwater and happens upon a big purple "thing." Why he chooses to use his laser cannon at this point is unclear. Surely, he could have relied upon his tried and true method of running away. Perhaps there were no rocks nearby ... it is a mystery. He decides to shoot the creature, instead. Though the creature has done him no harm, I think my 5 year old self would have argued that its large size and purple-ness warranted a preemptive strike.

Though largely accurate, the original tale only touches on some of the story's highlights. Important details were left out for various reasons. I have taken this opportunity to write ten volumes about what really happened. Keep reading, and enjoy!

MKS

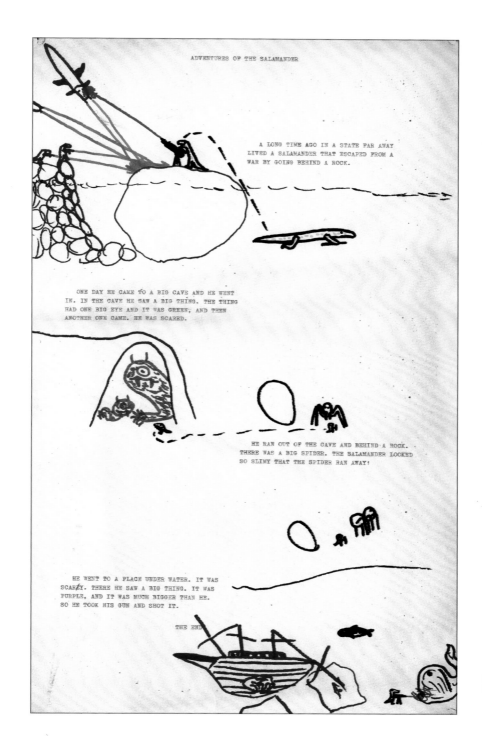

ADVENTURES OF THE SALAMANDER

A LONG TIME AGO IN A STATE FAR AWAY
LIVED A SALAMANDER THAT ESCAPED FROM A
WAR BY GOING BEHIND A ROCK.

ONE DAY HE CAME TO A BIG CAVE AND HE WENT
IN. IN THE CAVE HE SAW A BIG THING. THE THING
HAD ONE BIG EYE AND IT WAS GREEN, AND THEN
ANOTHER ONE CAME. HE WAS SCARED.

HE RAN OUT OF THE CAVE AND BEHIND A ROCK.
THERE WAS A BIG SPIDER. THE SALAMANDER LOOKED
SO SLIMY THAT THE SPIDER RAN AWAY!

HE WENT TO A PLACE UNDER WATER. IT WAS
SCARY. THERE HE SAW A BIG THING. IT WAS
PURPLE, AND IT WAS MUCH BIGGER THAN HE.
SO HE TOOK HIS GUN AND SHOT IT.

THE END

The Adventures of the Salamander

Volume 4: The Stark Mountains

THE ADVENTURES OF THE SALAMANDER
by Michael Klaus Schmidt

BOOK I • VOLUME 1

The Stark Mountains

Chapter 1: The Peak

The four companions, Slippy, Squeeks, Diggy, and Diggy's grandfather, or "Grandpa," as he was known, had been travelling upwards in the old rusty elevator for quite some time. Grandpa had brought some extra food and four canteens of water for their journey to the surface. A small pointer on top of the elevator door indicated that they were near the top of the shaft.

Slippy was on his way to Salamander Village, and the Stark Mountain elevator station was the closest to the village he could use. Slippy was desperate to get back home to his family and friends to fight the evil lizards that had taken over the village and bakery. On his journey to find help, he had unintentionally been sidetracked by one mishap after another; but now he was on his way home.

The anticipation was intense. For hours they had been stuck in the narrow, cramped space, and after several arguments had occurred, they had decided to remain quiet and to not talk to each other at all. Actually, it was Grandpa's suggestion; he realized it was the lack of space that made them get on each others' nerves. As they neared the top, all of them stared at the pointer, anxious to finish the ascent. Only Grandpa, who was whistling a pleasant tune, did not seem to mind the waiting.

Suddenly, a loud screech and an abrupt jerking of the chamber indicated that they'd reached the top. Cold mountain air rushed in to awaken the travellers' weary and cramped bodies. Squeeks let out a sigh of relief. Slippy rushed out through the door right behind Grandpa; he never wanted to see the inside of an elevator again, at least not for a long time. Diggy was relieved, but Grandpa seemed fine; he'd taken the trip on more than one occasion and was used to it.

Slippy looked around to take in the beautiful scenery. They were at the top of a mountain, surrounded by more mountains that seemed to stretch to the horizon and beyond. The air was clear and crisp, but the sky was dark and cloudy, and a cold breeze was blowing. The mountain peaks seemed to be domi-

Slippy, and his friends were stuck in the elevator for a long time. They rode from the center of the Earth all the way up to the Stark Mountains. They all wanted to get out, except Grandpa. Grandpa was very patient.

The elevator stopped on top of a mountain. After the long ride up, the travellers felt good to be able to breathe the fresh air and stretch their weary legs.

The view was beautiful. Slippy was excited, and happy to be so close to home ... until he heard a terrible noise.

nated by huge, gray rock formations with patches of short grass. Between them, one could see lush valleys with pine trees and the shimmering reflections of streams that ran down from the peaks. A trail led away from the elevator. In the distance, Slippy could see it bending around the side of the next mountain.

Turning back to his friends, Slippy noticed that the elevator exit was housed in a very small makeshift building with a triangular roof and a pipe sticking out of its side. Anyone looking would probably think it was just an outhouse*.

"Camouflage**!" said Grandpa, reading his thoughts. "We wouldn't want unwelcomed visitors down below. It's been a real pleasure to meet the both of you."

"Likewise," said Squeeks. "Thank you so much for your hospitality and all your help."

Slippy nodded in approval, "We would have been earth-wyrm food without you guys." Everyone agreed, and there was an abundance of hugging and shaking of hands.

Grandpa and Diggy had stepped into the elevator and were just about to head back down again when Squeeks suddenly heard a noise. It was a terrifying thudding sound that was getting louder and louder. Fumbling for words, he tried to alert the others, but by the time he could formulate a sentence, they had heard it too.

Grandpa looked visibly shaken. "Get out of the elevator!" he shouted at Diggy. Slippy looked around frantically, wondering where the noise came from. A scream escaping his lips, Squeeks pointed to something behind the elevator housing.

* An outhouse is a small building that houses a toilet.
** Camouflage is a way of hiding things to keep them from being discovered.

Then Slippy saw it, too, a huge figure that lurched over the brink of the mountain on which they stood.

Slippy was amazed by the size of the thing's head. It seemed disproportionately large for its body, which was huge, nonetheless.

Grandpa shouted, "Run!" and headed down the trail, wonderfully fast for an amphibian of his age. The others followed and hoped that the creature hadn't seen them.

Slippy could not help but look back to see what the thing was doing. It carried with it a huge iron sword, raising it above its head as it approached the elevator. Its head was not an ordinary head at all; it seemed to be a mass of hair and twigs, all writhing around.

Slippy could make out eyes and mouths and noses emerging from the mass of hair. It occurred to him that the creature did not have one big head; it had several heads ... more than one ... two heads ... no, there was another ... a three-headed giant! It was wearing some type of animal fur, held in place with a heavy belt. Its skin was grayish green and appeared to be made of stone, and the expression on its face suggested that it was not at all pleased with the existence of the elevator towards which it was lurching.

Suddenly, someone grabbed Slippy's arm; it was Grandpa. Squeeks and Diggy were about 100 yards farther down the trail, still running at a good pace. Grandpa gave Slippy a hard look and asked, "Do you really want to find out what's on the bottom of that troll's shoe?"

"A troll?!?" shouted Slippy as he ran, trying to stop imagining himself being squashed by the troll. They had reached a safe

A horrible three-headed troll came stomping over the mountainside towards the elevator. Slippy and his friends ran down the mountain path, hoping it hadn't seen them.

distance when they heard the crash, so Slippy thought it safe to turn and look. He saw that the troll had smashed its sword into the top of the elevator housing. Bits of metal and wood, springs and pulleys littered the ground where the elevator had been. Slippy saw what looked like a boy running away from the wreckage, but they were too far away to tell for sure.

Slippy turned back to see the troll smash the elevator to pieces with its huge sword. He also saw a boy running away from the elevator, getting away just in time.

All three heads of the troll roared at a deafening pitch, frightening Slippy and the others as they ran again, now even faster. When they looked back again for a quick glimpse, they saw the beast staggering back and forth trying to hold all three of its heads with its two hands. Apparently, it had hurt its own ears in the process of roaring like that.

They ran and ran for what seemed like hours, until Grandpa slowed down and turned back to see how far they'd come.

There was no sign of the troll; evidently, it had not seen them.

They let out a sigh of relief. Grandpa was the first to speak.

"Well, I guess you guys are stuck with Diggy and me now, with the elevator gone and all," he said. "But we were lucky; trolls are very dangerous when they're in a rage like that; they can squash any number of animals without even realizing it."

"I've never seen a troll before," said Squeeks, "but I've heard some terrible things about them."

"Well," said Grandpa, "some of those things are probably true."

Slippy added, "That thing had three heads ... or I'm a newt."

"Sure," said Grandpa, "some trolls have even more. Most only have one head, like you and me, but I've seen a troll with six heads."

"Six heads?!?" exclaimed Diggy and Squeeks.

"Oh, yes," continued Grandpa, "six heads, and as much hair as you please. But I've heard about even bigger trolls. They say there are trolls with twelve heads, the Troll Kings."

"Wow!" said Slippy, amused and scared at the same time. "I hope I never have to see such a troll; three heads was quite enough for me."

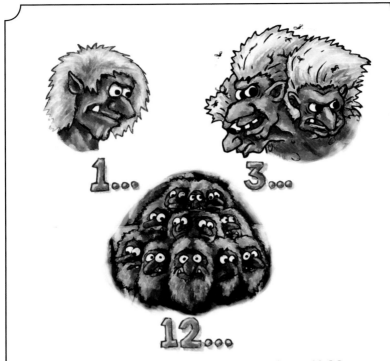

Grandpa told them about the different kinds of trolls. Some have one head, some three; the Troll Kings have as many as twelve heads.

Chapter 2: Twisting Trails

As they continued walking, the trail wound its way around the mountain. Suddenly, coming around a bend, the trail curved outwards and continued over a rocky bridge ... which appeared to come straight out of the side of the mountain; no supports held it up, and it seemed to defy gravity. Off it stretched until it reached the next mountainside, where the trail resumed its regular trail-like qualities. They were baffled, but Grandpa said it was safe to cross, advising that they be very careful not to lose their balance. There were no handrails to hold on to, and it could get rather windy up there in the mountains.

"I'm surprised such a bridge could stay up for very long," said Slippy, as he tried to hide the slight hint of fear in his voice.

"Oh sure," said Grandpa, "these bridges are made by gnomes, some of the finest craftsmen on the planet."

Slippy wondered if they would see any gnomes on their journey. As they came to the bridge, it turned out to be fairly

After escaping the troll, they reached a bridge that extended from one mountain to another. Grandpa said it must have been built by gnomes. Grandpa knew lots of stuff.

Coming around another mountain, they found an amazing set of bridges, called "The Twisting Trails," twisting and turning every which way. They crossed over a small river called "Clearmountain Stream."

wide, wide enough for a troll; there was little risk of them falling off as long as they stayed away from the edges. Once on the other side, the trail angled up to the right, around the next mountain.

It was slow going, and Slippy's feet were already tired, but not so bad as to require a rest just yet. Far away to the east, he noticed a faint rectangular light on a distant mountainside; it seemed to be getting narrower, and eventually it disappeared altogether.

When they came around another curve, they stopped to catch their breath in amazement. Just as the rays of the sun broke through the clouds, they saw ahead of them a great, deep valley, with many bridges like the one they had just crossed connecting one side to the other. These bridges were even more spectacular than the first. They twisted and turned every which way, even going around each other in a spiral at times. Here and there, some of the bridges met, creating a crossroad in mid-air. Slippy had trouble counting how many bridges there were, but he could see that the trail they were on seemed to meet up with several others on its way across the valley.

There also were a number of tunnels leading into the mountainsides, and, at the bottom of the valley, Slippy could see a beautifully clear mountain stream as it gently worked its way down to the lowlands.

Grandpa pulled a map out of his pack and sat down to study it. Slippy stood by him, taking the opportunity to have a closer look at the map.

"How do you read that?" asked Slippy.

"Oh, it's easy," explained Grandpa. "There are four main directions: north, south, east and west."

"I've heard of them," said Slippy, recognizing the terms.

"North is always at the top of the map, and south is at the bottom," clarified Grandpa. "East will be here, on the right, and west is over there, on the left." He explained while pointing to the appropriate sections of the map and towards the directions which they represented.

Slippy nodded, then had a closer look. He saw that the stream they had seen was called Clearmountain Stream; it flowed southeast, towards the Olde Forest. As it turned out, Grandpa learned there was indeed a trail that led southeast, roughly the same direction they were already heading. However, the trail they were on right now would eventually turn the wrong way.

Looking across the valley to the other side, Grandpa spotted the right trail. They figured out which bridge they needed to be on, and could see where it connected with another bridge, right in the middle of the valley. After a few slopes and turns, that other bridge wound around and connected with the bridge right in front of them.

"Easy as cave cricket pie!" said Grandpa.

Off they went, confident that they had done enough research to know where they were heading. As they started over the bridge, they passed several crossroads before the entire bridge curved around in a downward spiral, after which it connected with another bridge. Grandpa said that this was the one they needed, and they turned right to get onto it. There was only one more turn to make.

Slippy was not sure which way was which at this point, but

The Twisting Trails were so confusing that the travellers got totally lost. Instead of heading towards Salamander Village, they ended up going north, further into the mountains.

assumed that Grandpa knew. However, Grandpa was old and assumed that the younger Diggy would recognize the right direction and turn when it was time to turn. And yet, Diggy thought that Squeeks was the most worldly-wise of the bunch, having been a sailor and all, and was following him. Squeeks, on the other hand, felt that he was just along as Slippy's friend and was waiting for Slippy to tell them when to turn. In the end they arrived at the wrong trail. No one mentioned any-

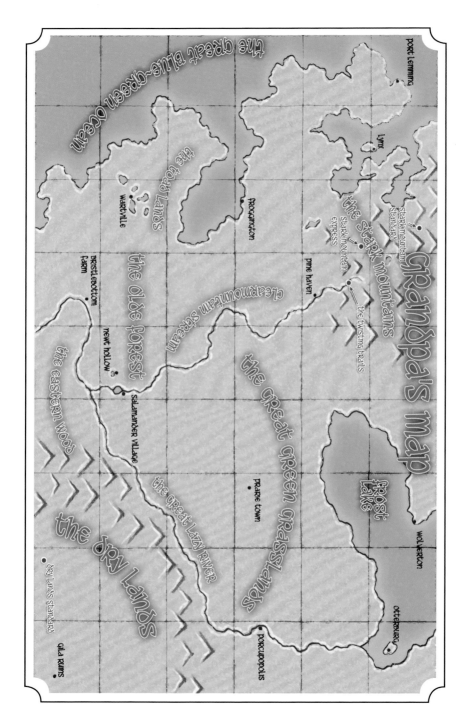

GRANDPA'S MAP

the great blue-green ocean

port lemming

lynx

stark mountains
standard

the toad lands

wartville

froggington

the stark mountains express

stark mountains

the stark mountains

pine haven

clearmountain stream

the twisting trails

bristlebottom farm

the olde forest

newt hollow

salamander village

frost lake

the great green grasslands

prairie town

wolverton

the eastern wood

the great lazy river

the dry lands

otterburg

porcupopolis

dry lands standard

gila ruins

160

> Looking at Grandpa's map, Slippy noticed that Clearmountain Stream flowed through the Olde Forest and into the Olde Slimy River. Slippy wondered why Clearmountain Stream was clear and fresh, but the Olde Slimy River was so dark and murky.

thing, though, each too embarrassed to admit that he didn't know which way was the right way.

The trail they were on now was actually going north, right into the heart of the Stark Mountain Range and not out of it, as they had hoped.

Grandpa finally broke the somewhat awkward silence, stating, "Got to love those gnomes! Building such amazing bridges as these!"

Everyone nodded in agreement and felt more confident by the second that they were heading down the right trail.

Chapter 3: The Troll Door

The trail led up the slope of a mountainside and wound around its peak, coming down the other side. From there, it crossed over another bridge, heading northwest and zigzagging along a bit. Finally, it came down through a valley where a pine forest grew. It was late afternoon when the team decided to make their camp.

Slippy was sent out to gather firewood; Squeeks was in charge of the food, you know, bugs and the like; Grandpa sat down to rest his wearied legs and study the map some more; and Diggy went out to find some fresh water for their canteens.

They all met back at the camp, started up a fire and roasted some of the bugs that Squeeks had caught on sticks. It was a great meal; far too long had it been since any of them had eaten anything decent. They drank fresh mountain water from the stream, cold as ice and clear as glass. It was some of the best water Slippy had ever had.

Having another look at Grandpa's map, Slippy was really surprised to find out that Clearmountain Stream, whose water he was drinking, must be the beginning of the Olde Slimy River. He could see that it flowed from the Stark Mountains right into Salamander Pond, where Salamander Village was clearly marked on the map.

"How," wondered Slippy, "could such a fresh, clear stream turn into the murky waters of the Olde Slimy River?" When he brought this to the attention of the group, they all shrugged and seemed somewhat puzzled themselves.

They decided to get some much deserved rest before heading out the next morning. Over the campfire they shared stories about all their adventures when Slippy saw another strange glowing rectangle on the side of a nearby mountain.

Grandpa told them everything he knew about trolls, including how they turn to stone if the sun shines upon them, and how their homes are made of gold.

They made camp for the night. While Slippy gathered wood, Squeeks found roly-polies to roast on the fire, and Diggy got some water to drink. Grandpa stayed at the camp and studied the map a bit more.

"The troll we saw," explained Grandpa, "was unusual, being out in the daylight like that. Sometimes they come out on cloudy days, but only for important reasons or if they're really upset."

He explained that there was a lot of misinformation about trolls, for example the idea that they ate animals and humans, or that they had brains the size of a pea. He explained that they were actually quite intelligent and that they ate mostly

As they sat around the campfire, eating and telling stories, Slippy saw a strange glowing rectangle on the side of a mountain.

potatoes, the roots of trees and rocks.

Grandpa noticed that Slippy had lost interest in the subject of trolls and seemed to be miles away in his thoughts. He sat down next to him to find out why: "What inspires such fierce concentration, Slippy?"

Slippy told him all the details about Salamander Village, the invasion by the lizards, his narrow escape, his many setbacks in his attempt to get back to save them. He wondered aloud about what he might do about the situation once he got there.

"I think we're here for a reason," said Grandpa; "it was no accident when that troll smashed the elevator. I think we're all here to help you get back home."

"No accident?" asked Slippy. "You mean it was somehow meant to be?"

"Sure," remarked Grandpa, "everything happens for a reason."

"But," continued Slippy, "does that mean that the lizards took over my village for a reason?"

"Everything," repeated Grandpa, "although the lizards probably aren't aware of it. All these things happen, good and bad, in order to help us find our purpose in life."

"Our purpose?" asked Slippy, slightly unsure.

"Exactly!" answered Grandpa, confidently. "Even though what the lizards did was wrong, it did serve to get you all the way out here to the Stark Mountains, didn't it?"

"I suppose so," said Slippy, "but what good is it? Here I am, stuck in these mountains, and I still see no way to save my family. How could being here be my purpose?"

"I'm not saying I know how, exactly," explained Grandpa, "but you did mention that you left your village to find help, right?"

"Sure," said Slippy.

"Well," said Grandpa, "look around you; you've got me, Squeeks and Diggy at your service' and you're not even home yet. Who knows whom we'll run into on the way down to your village."

They stayed up late, and Slippy spoke with Grandpa about Salamander Village. Grandpa said that there might be a good reason for Slippy's bad luck with the lizards. Grandpa always looked on the bright side.

"Hmmmm," said Slippy, "I guess so ..."

"If only we could fly, like birds," said Squeeks, "we'd get him home in no time."

"That reminds me!" said Grandpa, as he produced a long golden feather from his travel bag. "See this feather?" Everyone gazed at the beautiful feather in awe as Grandpa continued: "Fiona Flutterwing has been migrating South

through trog elevators for the last three seasons. She gave me this as a token of her appreciation just last Spring."
Squeeks asked, "Who's Fiona Flutterwing?"

"She's an old songbird, too old to make the trip South each year," explained Grandpa. "Birds around the world love her. Without the help of the trogs, she probably wouldn't have made it through the past three winters. Her tail feathers are worth more than gold among birds. They are given only to those whom she considers a 'Friend of Birds.'"

Everyone was impressed by the feather, but as dusk came upon the travellers, Grandpa suggested they put out the fire. There was no need to alert any trolls that they had visitors. They all agreed, and to make sure the embers no longer smoldered,

Later, Grandpa showed everyone his golden feather, which he got from a songbird who used the trog elevators. It was a beautiful feather, and it was a symbol that Grandpa was a "Friend of Birds."

they buried them in sand and dirt before going to bed. They slept in the hollow of an old tree, and all four of them were snoring within ten minutes.

At around midnight, strange noises woke Slippy from his dreams. Groggily, he opened his eyes and saw the Moon, still high in the sky, and heard a deep rumbling and scraping sound. On the mountainside right above, he saw the tiniest sliver of light. With another scrape, the line grew wider and slowly grew into a beautiful, golden rectangle of light. A shape appeared in its center, a huge hairy creature. It stood still for a moment and then strode out into the dark.

After they went to sleep, Slippy woke up to a strange noise. He saw another glowing shape on the mountainside ... and realized that it was a great big doorway.

"A door!" thought Slippy. "So that's where the trolls live, right inside the mountains!"

As carefully and quietly as he could, he got out of the hollow and climbed uphill to check out the strange door. He thought it best not to wake the others; they needed their rest, after all.

Once he reached the landing where the door was, he looked across the valley. He could see more mountains with more doors, some of which showed the silhouettes of more trolls heading into the night. Slippy though maybe he'd just have a peek inside, just a tiny peek ... and then he would get back to the camp as quickly as he could.

Chapter 4: A Golden Timepiece

The golden light seemed to come from the fireplace; Slippy remembered what Grandpa had told them about troll treasures, and he half expected to find gold inside. However, he was amazed at how well the troll lived; it had all the comforts of a modern home.

Through the doorway he could see what seemed to be a kitchen; he saw a great hearth with a huge pot for cooking nearby. There was a table with knives and forks and cleavers, used to prepare the troll's meals. Potatoes, carrots and other strange roots hung from ropes fastened to ceiling beams with nails. There were also several rocks and a tray of, what appeared to be grass, on the table. He began to wonder what a troll meal might actually taste like.

Slippy could see that the troll had several pairs of shoes lined up neatly against a wall. One pair was much smaller than the

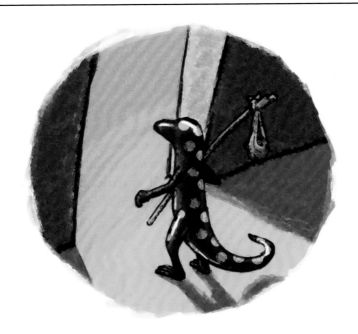

Slippy decided to find out what was behind the door. It turned out to be the home of a troll.

others, and he wondered what type of creature would keep its shoes from when it was a child. A broom rested in the corner, along with a great bellows, which was used for blowing the fire. A door led out of this room into a hall, and Slippy saw that there seemed to be several other rooms farther down.

"Psst!" Slippy heard a voice. "Hey, over here!" said the voice again. Slippy peered into the room, and, sure enough, there was a boy, a human boy, trapped in a cage next to the fireplace.

"Please help me!" the boy whispered.

Slippy cautiously entered the room and headed over to the cage, but it was locked with a large golden padlock. "What happened to you; are you okay?" Slippy asked the boy.

"I'm fine; I was caught by the troll," he stated, "almost got away, too."

Slippy was distraught; he wanted to help the poor lad, but there was no way to open the cage; it was far too strong. The boy laughed and took something out of his pocket, a golden timepiece.

"They didn't realize that I got this, though," he said, showing off the watch.

It somehow looked familiar to Slippy. "Did they steal that from you?" he asked.

"No," said the boy, "I stole it from them."

Slippy was confused; perhaps the trolls had done something bad to the boy or his family. "What did the trolls do?" he asked.

"The trolls?" said the boy.

"Yes, what did they do to make you feel like you needed to steal from them?" inquired Slippy.

"What do you mean?" asked the boy.

"I mean, why did you steal that golden timepiece from the trolls?" Slippy really began to wonder about the boy's mind.

"They're trolls!" said the boy, as if that was sufficient an expla-

A young boy named Hans was held
in a cage inside the troll's home. It
was the same boy Slippy had seen
by the elevator. He had been caught
trying to steal the troll's gold. He had
also stolen a pocket watch, which he
showed to Slippy.

nation.

Then it dawned on Slippy. He realized it was the same boy he
had seen running from the troll at the elevator.

Slippy was about to leave when he heard a noise. It was a cry,
like that of a baby, except louder and deeper than any baby
he'd ever heard. He turned around to see where it came from;

there in the hallway stood a large, hairy child, mouth wide open, pointing at Slippy. Of course! The shoes, the broom, the tidy kitchen ... the troll had a family, and this was the son.

Another larger troll came from one of the other rooms. Its long nose extended out from its face, which was mostly hidden behind the long frizzy hair that fell from its head. Grand-

The troll's wife surprised Slippy and found the pocket watch. She thought Slippy wanted to help Hans steal their gold, so she put him in the cage and went back to cooking.

pa would have noted that this was a troll hag, the wife of a troll, but he wasn't there at the moment. This one carried a large wooden spoon, the size of a small tree, and rushed over to the troll child to see what was the matter. The child pointed and cried again, and the troll hag looked over to where Slippy stood frozen next to the caged boy.

"So," said the troll hag in a deep, raspy, but clearly female voice, "here's your little accomplice, ready to help you escape?"

She saw the timepiece and grabbed Slippy as quickly as you can imagine.

Slippy tried to reason with her. "I'm not his accomplice; I was just looking, and I thought the boy needed help," he pleaded.

"Is that so?" asked the troll hag, as she placed Slippy gently into the cage with the boy. "Well, we'll let King Thrimple-bump decide that, won't we?" She plucked the timepiece out of the boy's hand, locked the cage and went about tidying up the kitchen.

Slippy and the human boy, whose name turned out to be Hans Bergman, had no choice but to anxiously wait. After a long time, Slippy asked the boy about the trolls and why he'd stolen the watch.

"Trolls have so much gold, they don't even know what to do with it," Hans answered.

"But it's their property, isn't it?" asked Slippy.

"Well, yeah, but they're trolls, they're monsters, and they eat humans, anyway," responded Hans.

Slippy began to feel like a detective as he inquired, "Have you ever seen a troll eat a human?"

"No," answered Hans.

"Did you ever know a human who was eaten by trolls?" Slippy questioned further.

"No, but my friend Ellie went missing a few months ago when she was up in the mountains, they must have eaten her!" answered Hans, somewhat defensively.

Slippy said, "I'm sorry to hear that, but how do you know for sure that they eat humans?"

"Everyone says so," said Hans quietly, "my grandma told me."

Suddenly, the light of dawn just started to illuminate the sky a tiny bit, and the door shut slowly. A huge hairy troll lumbered into the kitchen; it had three heads. As he sat down at the table, he demanded food, all three heads making the request.

The troll hag, who, by the way, only had one head, rushed in and prepared the table, serving what appeared to be huge potatoes and carrots, which had stewed in a pot all day. There were no bones or meat in the dish.

Slippy, hoping the trolls would hear him, shouted, "Excuse me!"

One of the troll's huge heads turned towards him; "Who's this?" he growled.

The troll hag explained what she'd seen earlier that night, and that she planned to take the both of them before King Thrim-

Slippy and Hans were worried that the trolls would eat them. They watched with fear, as the troll hag, made some sort of stew. When the troll came home he was in a bad mood, and very hungry ...

... but surprised to find Slippy there. The troll said they would not eat Hans or Slippy, but would take them to the Troll King, to be tried for stealing. Trolls liked to think they were fair.

plebump for a judgment.

The troll asked, "Did you see the salamander trying to help the boy escape?" Another one of his heads seconded the request: "Yeah, did you see it?"

"No," explained its wife.

"Well, did you catch the salamander with some of our gold?" asked the troll's third head.

"No," said the troll hag, quieter this time.

The troll then turned to Slippy and asked, "Are you and this thief working together?"

They both answered, "No."

The huge troll got up from its dinner and stomped over to the cage Slippy and Hans were in; he lifted the cage and unlatched its door. He then gently picked up Slippy and put him down on the floor.

"Well," he began, "would you show me the contents of your bag, just to clear up any doubts my wife has?"

Slippy said, "All right, Sir." But as he said it, he remembered the golden timepiece he'd been given back on Golden Leaf Island. As he opened the bag, he closed his eyes and hoped that they would not think he had stolen theirs.

"Hmmm," said the troll, seeing the timepiece, "where did you get this?"

The troll hag shouted, "Aha! I knew he was a thief!"

The trolls found out that Slippy had the exact same pocket watch as the one Hans had stolen. This was very strange; Slippy could not explain it. He was worried that they might think he had stolen his too ...

"Not so fast," said the troll, "I only had one timepiece; and you said the boy had that one, right?"

"Yes, I suppose he did," said the troll hag, "but they look exactly the same!"

Sure enough, the two timepieces looked identical to one another. This made Slippy very confused, and he started to panic.

"I got it on Golden Leaf Island, at the Marketplace," he explained. "It was given to me by ... somebody." He couldn't remember exactly how he'd gotten it.

The troll looked at both timepieces and said, "Well, I'm a bit confused by this, too, but since we caught the boy trying to steal our golden spoons, it's likely that he was also the one who stole the timepiece."

He turned to Hans and asked, "Where did you get the other golden timepiece?"

... But the Troll, whose name was "Crumblesticks," knew that Slippy could not have stolen the watch. He only had one watch to begin with.

Hans looked down, ashamed to admit the truth, but he did not want to get Slippy into any trouble, either.

"It was yours; I stole it," he said. "The salamander had nothing to do with it."

The troll gave Slippy both timepieces and said, "Here you go; that's for any trouble we've caused you. Now you have two."

Slippy thanked them and put both timepieces back into his bag.

Chapter 5: The Troll King

The trolls let Slippy leave, but not before the troll hag had given him a large potato to take along. He carried it all the way down to where he had left his friends. When he arrived back at the hollow tree, he found his friends still asleep. He woke them up, and they all ate the huge potato for breakfast. Slippy explained what had happened, and Grandpa seemed keenly interested in the tale.

When Slippy produced the golden timepieces to show them, the troll's appeared to be the exact same as the one the wizened old salamander (who Slippy had forgotten about) had given him so long ago on Golden Leaf Island. When he compared the two, they even had the same tiny scratches on the lens. What were the chances that he would receive two identical timepieces? It was all too baffling to think about; maybe his friends had an explanation. All of them were in awe at their beauty and precision.

"Gnomes made those," said Grandpa. "That gives me an idea!"

The trolls let Slippy go, giving him the second watch for his troubles. When Slippy returned to the camp, he had two pocket watches ... and a story to tell.

After cleaning up their campsite, the four travellers climbed up the ridge to where the troll door was. Slippy knocked on the door, and, after a few moments, it opened up a tiny bit.

The troll hag asked, "Who is it?"

"It's me, Slippy, the Salamander," said Slippy.

"Oh, come in," answered the hag, who could not come out from behind the door due to the sunlight.

When Grandpa heard Slippy's story about the trolls and Hans, he had an idea. He decided to come along to the trial because he thought he could help the trolls and humans live in peace. Grandpa liked to help people.

Slippy and his three companions went inside, and the door was quickly shut behind them. There stood the troll hag, smiling down at them. Hans was still in the cage, wrapped in a blanket and sleeping.

Grandpa was the first to speak, "I have a proposition for you, Ma'am." He began to explain that he would like to accompany the boy Hans when he went before the Troll King.

"Why?" she asked.

Grandpa explained, "I think I have an idea, something that will help you get along with the humans better."

"Oh, that'll be the day!" exclaimed the hag. "Humans and trolls, getting along! Ha!" She laughed a deep grunting laugh for a long time.

Her husband must have woken up when she laughed because he came into the kitchen. When he saw the salamander, the mouse and two trogs, he looked genuinely pleased. He introduced himself: "I'm Troll Crumblesticks" (that was the proper way of saying a troll's name); "we'll be glad to have you as guests to the Troll King's court," he said.

Along the way, Slippy learned more about trolls. Trolls lived in mountains; their homes were along the outer surface. Each home, however, was connected by well-lit passageways to a great central chamber where they would have parties and engage in other community activities like weddings, birthdays and court cases. The Troll King would travel from one mountain community to the next within his realm, spending a week out of every month away from his palace, which was located in the largest mountain near the center of his kingdom.

When visiting other communities, he would judge cases for the trolls under his dominion, and they would take the chance to serve him great boiled potatoes and soup and have their human captives scratch his hairy, bug-infested heads. The trolls explained that this would probably be the fate of young Hans, for it was the punishment for thievery.

Grandpa asked if he might have the chance to speak with the Troll King about this.

"Yes," said Troll Crumblesticks, "the King hears all suggestions and complaints when visiting, even from our guests."

"He must be a truly wise king," replied Grandpa. "Can I ask, what's the punishment for stealing in troll law?"

"Oh, the boy will become our head scratcher, of course," said Troll Hag Crumblesticks (that's the proper way to say a troll hag's name).

Hans let out a wimper when he heard this, just as they arrived in the hall. It contrasted sharply with the homes of the troglodytes; most of the stone tables and chairs were huge, but there were other, smaller tables, too. It also had no sign of the modern machinery that the trogs held so important. Trolls and numerous other creatures gathered around a huge throne. On the throne sat an enormously fat troll, bigger than Troll Crumblesticks ... it was Troll-King Thrimplebump (that's the proper way to say a troll king's name) himself.

Twelve heads sat upon his gigantic shoulders, and shaggy hair and beards grew in every direction. His hair was filled with the oddest assortment of sticks and leaves; birds' nests appeared to have been built in some of his ears, and a swarm of flying insects seemed always to be hovering around him.

In one corner of the room sat a young girl, looking very sad. Troll Crumblesticks mentioned that she was the Troll King's head scratcher. Hans was very surprised to see her; it was Ellie, who had gone missing months before. Everyone thought she'd been eaten. He was happy to see her but terrified that her fate would be his too.

Troll-King Thrimplebump was a huge,
twelve-headed troll. He ruled over the
trolls of the Stark Mountains and was
about to judge Hans. If found guilty,
Hans would have to become Troll
Crumblesticks's head scratcher.

In a corner of the Troll-King's hall sat a girl. She was the Troll King's head scratcher and she looked very sad. Hans knew her from his village; her name was Ellie. He wondered how he might save her, and he wished he had never stolen any gold from the trolls.

A long line of trolls waited before Thrimplebump's throne, each with its own problems and issues to ask of the King. Troll Crumblesticks and his wife got in line and waited, as well.

Slippy looked around the hall some more, and noticed several other small creatures that looked nothing like trolls. They were much shorter, with long beards and funny hats. Some of them waited in line as they carried trinkets of gold and gems as an offering for the King. Others sat at the tables with trolls and ate along with them. Still others served food to those seated at the tables.

"Gnomes," said Grandpa, noticing that Slippy had seen them. They were about as tall as Hans and seemed quite jolly and talkative.

Before long, Grandpa, Troll Crumblesticks and Hans stood in front of Troll-King Thrimplebump, while Slippy, Diggy and Squeeks enjoyed some of the tomato-potato soup the gnomes were bringing around to each table. Trolls and gnomes are very fond of tomato-potato soup, and Slippy understood why right away: it was delicious!

They met a very nice gnome named Gnorman* who brought them their soup. But before they could ask him any questions, he said, "Shhhhhh, the Troll-King is about to judge the boy."

"Greetings, my troll subjects," began Thrimplebump. "How can I be of service to you today?" He spoke in a very formal manner.

Troll Crumblesticks shook the King's hand and began to present his case against Hans.

"The boy tried to steal our golden timepiece and our golden spoon collection," began Troll Crumble-sticks; "we caught him red-handed."

"That's a very serious charge," said the King to Hans. "Do you have anything to say for yourself?"

* Pronounced "Norman."

Hans was so frightened, he could not speak.

"Since you do not wish to defend your actions," continued the King, "we hereby hold that you are guilty. Your punishment will be to scratch Troll Crumblesticks' heads for the rest of your life."

Hans wept; he had known it would happen. It was the worst moment of his life.

Chapter 6: An Unexpected Reunion

"Excuse me!" said Grandpa. "I have a complaint that relates to this case!"

Troll-King Thrimplebump looked around, trying to find the source of the voice.

"Down here!" shouted Grandpa. The Troll King looked down to see the old troglodyte.

"Ah, yes," said Troll-King Thrimplebump, "how can we help you?"

"It seems," began Grandpa sternly, "that some troglodyte property has been destroyed by one of the plaintiffs* in this case."

Crumblesticks looked as if he'd just swallowed a small boulder.

"Proceed," said the King. By this time, all the trolls and gnomes in the hall were listening intently.

"Well, it seems," continued Grandpa, "that Troll Crumbles-

* A plaintiff is the person who is stating a complaint in a trial, in this case, troll Crumblesticks.

When Hans was on trial before the Troll-King, Grandpa stood up to help him. Meanwhile Slippy, Diggy and Squeeks met a friendly gnome named Gnorman who served them some yummy tomato-potato soup.

ticks, in his effort to catch young Hans, went about smashing one of our elevators."

"I see!" said the King, almost all of his heads turning towards Crumblesticks. "Do you have anything to say about this?"

"Ummm, I ... er ... no?" said Troll Crumblesticks. Six of the King's faces looked with disapproval at Crumblesticks, while

Grandpa argued with the Troll-King. When Grandpa told him about the elevator that Troll Crumblesticks had destroyed, the King agreed to let Hans go free. Hans would not have to become a head scratcher! Grandpa was good at making peace.

the other six nodded at Grandpa, and said "We would be happy to pay for the rebuilding of the elevator."

Grandpa shook his head; "We'll take the boy."

A hush fell over the crowd, followed by murmurs of "That's

unheard of!" and "How dare they!" and "There's no precedent!"

The King silenced them with a wave of his hand and said "This has nothing to do with the human child; you will need to ask for something else."

"But it does," replied Grandpa. "The humans have been told stories about trolls all their lives. They think that trolls eat humans, and how are they to know any differently? Every time they're captured, you make them your servants, and their families never see them again. They assume that they've been eaten; how could they not?"

"But that's wrong," replied the King; "we don't eat them, and we only capture those who have been trespassing on our land, out to steal our gold, no doubt."

"Yes, but how would they know? Don't you think you could make an exception sometimes?" pleaded Grandpa. "Don't you think you could let this one go, for the sake of kindness? He's only a child. He'll go home and tell his family that trolls don't eat humans, and that you're far more intelligent than they'd guessed. The humans might realize that it's wrong to steal from you too. Give it a chance."

The Troll King pondered this new argument. All twelve of his heads looked truly perplexed. After a long silence, he responded, "The boy may go!"

Cheers rose up from the crowd of trolls and gnomes in the hall, because trolls like nothing more than true justice. Slippy was happy, too, and he saw that, as Hans released a smile of relief, a tear rolled silently down each of his cheeks.

After a wonderful meal, Slippy, Grandpa, Squeeks, Diggy and young Hans talked for a few hours with the trolls and gnomes, but eventually the time came for kind words and many handshakes as the two groups parted ways. Slippy took down the recipe for tomato-potato soup and promised Gnorman he would tell all his friends and family about it. Gnorman thanked him for his kindness and told them all to keep in touch.

They went out through a different door than the one they'd come in; Gnorman had told them how to get to the right trail from there. Slippy and the others felt foolish; they still hadn't even considered they might be on the wrong trail at all. When they came out, it was still early; the sky was bright, and they saw the new trail heading down into a valley. This one met up with the southeastern trail that they thought they had been on.

The trail led to Pine Haven where they planned to drop off Hans with his family before they made their way out of the mountains. As they crossed over a ridge, Slippy saw a flag coming up from the other side. He thought it might be the top of a tower, but quickly noticed that the "tower," too, gradually moved upwards. It was attached to a large round object of some sort, which also rose higher and higher.

The whole group stopped, wondering what new horror was being revealed to them. Attached to the bottom of the large round object was some kind of ship. In the ship, Slippy could see two figures: one was a large furry animal; the other one looked like a shelled reptilian.

As it drew closer, Slippy saw that the device before them hovered above the ground. Its elaborate clockwork mechanism consisting of a complex assortment of gears, cables and pulleys

After the trial, Gnorman gave Slippy his recipe for tomato-potato soup. He also showed them how to get back on the right trail. They took Hans along with them, and they hoped the trolls and humans might be nicer to each other in the future.

powered what appeared to be rotating fins, which propelled the machine through the air. A wooden platform, which looked kind of like a boat, allowed passengers to stand aboard the craft; and the large round shape at the top was some sort of lighter-than-air balloon that kept the whole thing aloft.

"Slippy!" cried the reptile aboard the craft. Slippy recognized the face as it came closer.

After leaving the trolls, Slippy and his friends were rescued by Sheldon and Captain Bigsby in a flying machine. They began their voyage back to Salamander Village ... but that's another story.

"Sheldon?" he shouted back, though he could hardly believe it to be true. How could they have found him here?

Mr. Bigsby, the platypus, turned out to be the captain of this strange vehicle. He called it "The Fanciful Flying Machine," and the name fit it well. Sheldon and Captain Bigsby, as he liked to be called when flying, landed, and they were introduced to Slippy's other friends. More handshakes and kind greetings were exchanged than are worth mentioning here.

Then they all climbed aboard the airship and began a presumably much shorter voyage back home. Slippy was relieved; he was finally on his way home.

Little did he know ... but that's another story.

Appendix II: Tomato-Potato Soup

This was the soup recipe that Slippy retrieved from the gnome Gnorman. Tomato-Potato Soup was thus brought out of its birthplace in the Stark Mountains down into the Olde Forest.

As a result, the terrapins of Golden Leaf Island were introduced to it, and they began selling it at the Marketplace on the west side of Golden Leaf Island to the traders who came from all over the world.

Tomato-Potato Soup became a world-wide phenomenon thereafter, being adopted by cultures all over the world. Many nations brought their own ideas and ingredients into the recipe, and it evolved into many exciting and delicious soups. However, controversy arose when various groups claimed the recipe as their own.

For instance, the Mice on the Western Isles added a cheese topping to the soup but insisted that it had been part of their culture for centuries. Later, a popular variant involving dried lichen came from Port Lemming in the north. The Lemmings tried to convince everyone that they had given the recipe to the gnomes during one of their great pilgrimages.

Some scholars continue to debate this matter to this very day. I'm happy to be able to contribute my findings. The original document, reproduced here, should help settle the matter once and for all.

MKS

RECIPE: Gnorman's Famous Tomato-Potato Soup

Ingredients:
1 can of tomato soup (brand of your choosing)
2 or 3 ~~Kartoffeln~~ potatoes (peeled & cut into small chunks)
1 onion, diced (optional)
1/2 teaspoon of Basil (fresh)

Directions:
Brown onions in a dab of butter in medium size pot. Pour soup into pot, adding 1 can of water, if required. Add potatoes and bring to a boil. Sprinkle basil on soup and allow to cook on low heat for at least one hour, stirring occasionally.

Soup will be hot, so allow time for it to cool down.
Serve and enjoy!

Sincerely,
Gnorman

Dear Reader,

I hope you have as much fun reading about Slippy's adventures as I enjoyed writing about them. Meet Slippy's friends, encounter strange creatures, and see the unusual and exotic places he visits in his efforts to return home to save his family.

For parents: This story is written for children of all ages. under each picture, I've added detailed captions that tell the whole story in an easy-to-understand way for younger children. Older kids and adults can enjoy the full story and learn all the details that are not included in the captions. Footnotes, maps and appendices are included for those who want to investigate further.

Enjoy,

Michael Klaus Schmidt

The Adventures of the Salamander is also available as digital ebooks on Amazon.com Kindle Store.

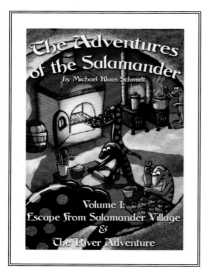

VOLUME 1:
ESCAPE FROM SALAMANDER VILLAGE

Salamander Village is overrun by mean-spirited lizards. Slippy the Salamander must do something to save his family and friends, who are being forced to bake for the lizards. Find out how Slippy escapes. On his way out of the Village, Slippy meets a terrapin named Sheldon whose family may be able to help. Find out what happens when they travel down the river to Golden Leaf Island.

VOLUME 2:
SAILING THE GREAT BLUE-GREEN OCEAN

While trying to find Sheldon's father, Mr. Schumacher, at the Market Place, Slippy gets stuck on Captain Crap-Apple's ship, the "Sea Serpent." Find out what happens when he sails the Great Blue-Green Ocean, how he meets his friend Squeeks and what they do when they run into pirates. What tragedy will befall them on the Skull Islands?

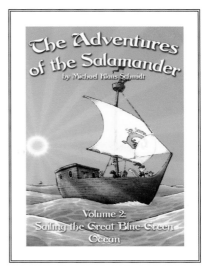

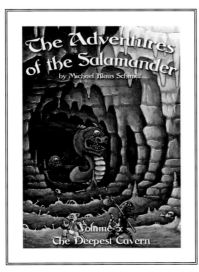

VOLUME 3:
THE DEEPEST CAVERN

Slippy the Salamander and Squeeks the Mouse are stuck at the bottom of "The Hole." Find out what they discover when they climb down into the Deepest Cavern to escape from the "Earth-Wyrms." What will they do to get back to the surface, and who will help them?

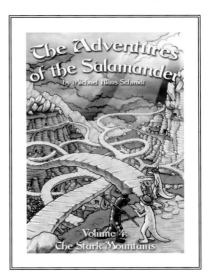

VOLUME 4:
THE STARK MOUNTAINS

Slippy, Squeeks, Diggy and Grandpa arrive by elevator in the Stark Mountains, home of twisting paths and frightening trolls. Find out what happens when they get lost on the way to Salamander Village, and how they encounter the trolls, confront the Troll King and rescue Hans. And learn who shows up, unexpectedly, right out of the clear, blue sky?

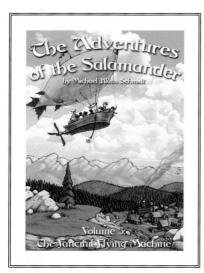

VOLUME 5:
THE FANCIFUL FLYING MACHINE

When Slippy, Squeeks, Diggy and Grandpa are rescued by Sheldon and Captain Bigsby in an airship, they think it will be easy to get back home. Find out what they discover about the Olde Slimy River, which strange structures they find hidden in the clouds, whom they befriend and how they solve their dilemma.

VOLUME 6:
THE LUNAR EXCURSION

After our friends climb up the Golden Ladder, they meet the Great Aviatrix. Who is she, what does she look like, and why did she lead them to the Moon? Find out what happens when they reach her castle, what danger they are in and who comes to their rescue.

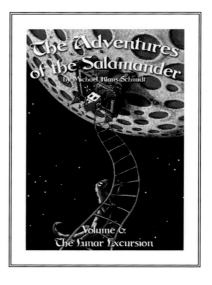

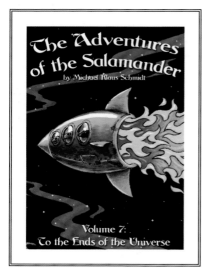

VOLUME 7:
TO THE ENDS OF THE UNIVERSE

Slippy, Squeeks, Diggy, Grandpa, Sheldon and the Rocket Baron set out back to Earth in the Rocket Baron's rocket ship. Find out what happens when the Rocket Baron makes a "slight miscalculation" in the rocket's course and they end up travelling to the Ends of the Universe. Where will they land, what strange creatures will they meet, and how will they get back?

VOLUME 8:
THE TRAVELLER OF TIME

When Slippy is left behind on the planet Trillak, Smortlex, his Trillakian friend, gives him a time travelling machine to help him save the Salamanders. Find out how his village has changed, how difficult it is to change the past ... and what he can do about changing the future.

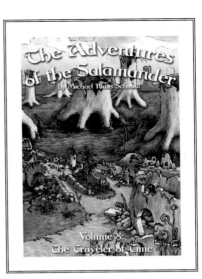

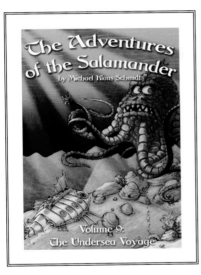

VOLUME 9:
THE UNDERSEA VOYAGE

When Squeeks, Diggy, Grandpa, Sheldon and the Rocket Baron arrive back on Earth, they crash-land at the bottom of the Great Blue-Green Ocean. Can Slippy save them, and will they survive their encounter with the Krak-O-Pod? Find out how Slippy unexpectedly finds the purpose of his life.

VOLUME 10:
THE WAY BACK HOME

Reunited with his friends, equipped with a newly found courage, and captaining his own undersea device, Slippy is ready to return home and save Salamander Village. Find out what happens when they finally arrive. Can they overcome the lizards, who will help them and who has betrayed them all along? What skills will Slippy need to convince everyone that the lizards are up to no good?